I0679822

SKINWALKER

SKINWALKER

GIDEON THORN
BOOK 1

MICHAEL NEWTON

Skinwalker
Paperback Edition
Copyright © 2025 (As Revised) by Michael Newton

Dark Wolf Books
An Imprint of Wolfpack Publishing
1707 E. Diana Street
Tampa, FL 33610

www.darkwolfbooks.com

All rights reserved. No part of this book may be reproduced in any form or by any electronic or mechanical means, including information storage and retrieval systems, without express written permission from the publisher, except for the use of brief quotations in reviews. Any use of this publication to train generative artificial intelligence (AI) technologies is expressly prohibited.

This book is a work of fiction. References to historical events, real people, or real places are used fictitiously. Any similarity to real persons, living or dead, is purely coincidental and not intended by the author.

All brand names and product names used in this book are trademarks, registered trademarks, or trade names of their respective holders. Wolfpack Publishing is not associated with any product or vendor in this book.

Paperback 979-8-89567-936-4
Ebook 979-8-89567-933-3

SKINWALKER

PROLOGUE

KANSAS TERRITORY: NOVEMBER 1854

A howling rips the snow-shot darkness, ululating on the wind that blows down from the Rockies, looming westward. "There it is again," his mama says.

The toddler can't remember whether he has heard the sound before. He only knows it frightens him.

It scares his parents, too, a sudden sense of insecurity the toddler does not understand. His papa has the long gun down from where he keeps it, hung above the mantelpiece. His mama stands a pace behind her man, holding her carving knife. The toddler's older brother, Tommy, stands beside his bed, a chopper in his hand. At first, the toddler thinks it's meant for him, but then his brother turns away to face their parents, both on station now between the two boys and the door.

The howling is repeated, closer, no way to mistake it for the moaning of the storm. His parents do not speak, but he can see his mama trembling, not from cold, since they have built a roaring blaze inside the stone fireplace. His father has the long gun shouldered now, aiming it as if he's threatening the night outside.

The first animate sound against their door is snuffling, followed by a scratching noise. They do not have a dog, and yet the toddler instinctively pictures a set of claws raking the outer wood, testing its strength. Next up, a rumbling growl and more determined scrabbling.

"Aaron?" says his mama.

"Hush, Felicity!" his papa answers back through gritted teeth.

A great force strikes the door, beyond the awesome power of the wind. The toddler sees it bow inward against the six-foot bar restraining it. His brother edges backward till he bumps against the bed and can retreat no further without crawling underneath, a feat his self-respect will not permit.

More scratching in a kind of frenzy now, making the door tremble within its frame. The toddler fears to see long splinters peeling from the inside, but before that happens, sudden silence falls outside. His mind grasps at a hope: perhaps the thing, whatever *it* is, has decided that it cannot breach their home.

He waits, afraid to crack the silence with his voice, until he hears a sound like hoofbeats rushing toward them, galloping, and something strikes the door with a tremendous force, snapping its heavy bar it two, flinging the door itself wide open on the night. A blast of snow whips through the one-room cabin, and a hulking shape crosses the threshold, somehow darker than the night outside.

The lamps go dark in unison, only the fireplace left to light the slaughterhouse.

The toddler sees and hears his papa fire the long gun, muzzle flash leaping to scorch the ceiling as his aim is spoiled, the shadow-shape attacking him. His stocky, so familiar shape goes flying to the left and strikes a wall of logs, collapsing to the floor. The toddler's mama screams something he cannot comprehend and strikes out with her knife. A massive arm or paw sweeps her aside, off toward the hearth.

That leaves his brother as the last line of defense. Tommy stands fast, armed with his chopper, spitting words their papa sometimes says but children are admonished not to echo. As the shadow-thing approaches now, slowly and rumbling in its chest, Tommy rears back, prepares to strike and make the first blow count.

In the event, though, he has no more chance than either of their elders. When the hand-paw strikes him down, a crimson mist speckles the toddler's face and his blue home-made pajamas, warm on contact, one thick streamer nearly covering his left eye altogether. Tommy's there, and in the next heartbeat he's gone, as if he were a passing fantasy.

And now the creature looms over the toddler's bed. He half-sees amber eyes regarding him with what he takes for hunger and a hint of curiosity. The shaggy, lumbering intruder stretches out the same limb that obliterated Tommy, reaching for him with its long, curved claws.

One talon's tip traces a line of fire across the toddler's scalp from crown to hairline, opening the flesh enough to start his own blood flowing—then a miracle occurs. His mama rushes forward, trailing flames behind her from the fireplace, and she's found the carving knife or maybe never dropped it, long blade plunging into fur and sinew while she strikes repeatedly, screaming her rage.

The creature—is it safe to call it *monster,* when his parents say that no such things exist?—turns back to face her with a snarl, rising or seeming to until its head brushes the cabin's ceiling, flattening its pointed ears. The toddler's mama holds her ground, the long knife slashing, jabbing, but he understand the words she's shouting now.

"Run, Gideon! For God's sake, run!"

He doesn't think about it, rolls out of the bed bare-footed, snatching at the quilted coverlet before he hits the floor. He smells the looming creature, something feral, as he flits behind it, clears the room that is the only home he knows, and gains its only exit.

Rushing out into the storm-swept night.

ONE

Gideon Thorn surveyed the wolf pack through the long scope mounted on his Sharps rifle, counting eleven individuals. The smallest of the gray wolves, these had roots in Mexico's Sierra Madre—"Mother Mountains"—fanning out from there across America's Southwest. Because they posed no threat to Thorn or either of his animals, he opted not to thin their numbers from afar.

They weren't the creatures that he hunted, anyway.

It was a long ride north from Ciudad de Hermosillo in Sonora, Mexico, Thorn's last stop on the endless loop of his itinerary. There, he had investigated stories of a *bruja* operating in the neighborhood but found no evidence of any witches operating in Sonora's capital. Locals had humored him—a *gringo* chasing superstition, wasting time for all concerned—and helped him understand that yellow journalists had blown a simple story out of all proportion, fabricating most of it to suit their editors in the United States.

When the chaff was winnowed out, Thorn traced the "witchcraft" to an aged crone who sold folk remedies at bargain prices, usually being paid with simple offerings of food. A stringer for Chicago's *Daily Journal,* tramping around Mexico to write a series on that nation's progress since expulsion of French occupying forces eight years earlier, had fastened on the basics of the *bruja* rumor and embellished to his heart's content. The tale had grown from there, repeated with elaborations from New York to San Francisco by so-called reporters who had never crossed the Río Grande, much less investigated any details of the story prior to adding nonsense of their own.

In short, there was no witch, no demonology of any kind.

This time.

Gideon Thorn had traveled some four hundred fifty miles to chase that fantasy, starting in San Diego, California. Riding a horse, trailing a pack mule with four miles per hour taken as a lucky average, the trip had taken him eleven days, including Thorn's passage across the Río Sonora. He had come through all of that intact but had nothing to show for it, and now he was returning to the States, northeastward, traveling about five hundred sixty miles to Tularosa. Crossing the Sierra Madre Occidental, call it two weeks minimum to reach his secondary destination.

And for what?

More clippings, turning yellow, creased along their folds where Thorn had studied them almost to tatters. Given his photographic memory, only a single reading was required, but he pored over them by campfire light and in the odd hotel room while he traveled, as if hoping some new bit of knowledge would present itself.

Tularosa was a village in Otero County, named like its

surrounding basin for rose-colored reeds sprouting along the Río Tularosa's banks. Its eastern boundary faced the Sacramento Mountains, a range stretching eighty-five miles east to west above flat, arid desert. Mexican farmers from the Río Grande had been driven out by Apache raiders in 1860, then returned to defeat them at nearby Round Mountain in 1862, establishing the Town of Tularosa one year later. Whites had followed, as they always did, and staked out ranches for themselves as far as they could reach.

Now someone or some*thing* was killing people around Tularosa, and the slaughter had been going on for months. Gideon Thorn hoped to discover how and why.

He came prepared. Besides the Sharps—the 1872 model chambered in .50-90 caliber, accurate to fifteen hundred yards with its custom-made, three-foot-long scope—Thorn also carried a Winchester Model 1873, a lever-action repeater chambered in .44-40, with fifteen rounds in its tubular magazine and one in its chamber. His gunbelt supported a matched pair of Colt Single Action Army revolvers, the famed "Peacemaker," produced in the same year as his Winchester and in the same caliber, to conserve ammunition. Should all else fail, he wore a twelve-inch Bowie knife and packed a smaller dagger, double-edged, in the top of his right knee-high boot.

Well armed, Thorn also struck an imposing appearance. From head to toe he dressed in midnight black, now dusty from the trail: his wide-brimmed, high-crowned hat; his frock coat and vest; his trousers tucked into the knee-high black boots. The sole hint of relief in Thorn's attire was his white shirt, and even that was solemnized by a black string tie. When he removed the hat, another streak of shocking white parted his raven hair, tracking a scar that crossed his scalp from hairline to the crown.

Gideon Thorn resembled someone en route to a funeral, although the last one he'd attended had occurred nearly two years ago.

As for the next one, it had not been scheduled yet.

He'd missed the burials at Tularosa, spanning the past sixteen months, but they were all duly recorded in the articles he carried, totaling a baker's dozen dead so far.

The first to die, on February 2, 1874, were Frank and Judith Carmody, residing on a farm nine miles northwest of town. When they had missed their standard Saturday appointment to join neighbors for the trip to buy supplies in Tularosa, curiosity won out and they were found at home, both butchered in the manner of an animal attack. Discretion barred the press from giving details, but the articles in Thorn's collection said both man and wife were grossly mutilated, one item referring to dismemberment. Otero County's sheriff blamed a wolf pack, wound up shooting half a dozen feral dogs, and thought he'd solved the problem for his loyal constituents.

Almost precisely four weeks later, on March 3, young lovers Marlon Spence and Betty Lou Paulson slipped off to find some privacy midway between their parents' farms, six miles southwest of Tularosa. Both were missed at breakfast and a search began, discovering their torn, scattered remains by half-past noon. This time, reporters mentioned gnawing on the bodies, claw marks, and apparent disembowelment, though some of the injuries might have been caused post-mortem, by coyotes.

April passed without an incident, while Tularosans held their breath and waited for the next grim news. By May 1 they had started to relax, hoping the unknown killer had moved on to other hunting grounds, but their relief was premature. That afternoon, broad daylight, fifteen-year-old

Joe Margulies had gone to feed his family's hogs, penned up a hundred yards from their farmhouse. When he had not returned by dusk, Joe's father went to check and found most of his eldest son—some of him in the hog pen, other bits and pieces scattered up and down the outside of the split rail fence. Joe's left leg, missing from the scene, had yet to be accounted for.

So far, all of the slayings coincided with full moons, and May had two, the only month that year to herald a "blue moon." That night, May 31, four members of the Ostman family were savaged in their farmhouse, six miles west of Tularosa. Sole survivor of the massacre was six-year-old Justine Ostman, who had gone to use the backyard privy shortly after midnight. Thus engaged, she heard her kinfolk screaming from the house but dared not go to look, much less to aid them. If her parents and two older brothers could not save themselves, what help was she to them? Next morning, at the crack of dawn, she'd walked two miles to reach the nearest neighbor's spread and asked for help. The search revealed a nightmare scene, and the first evidence of an attack indoors by what the county's sheriff still referred to as an animal.

How had it used the front door's knob, Thorn wondered, when it crept into the house? And having done its gruesome work, how did it use a bedroom window to escape? Doubts not withstanding, though, the bloody tracks it left behind revealed some kind of *paws,* not human feet. It's rending of the walls and furniture bespoke a fearsome set of claws.

June passed with Tularosa still in shock. July was little better, but again, its full moon passed without more bloodletting. Come August, once again, numbed villagers had dared to think beyond their fear and superstition, had ceased huddling in their two churches on every possible occasion, when disaster struck on Thursday the twenty-seventh. Brothers Brent and Cabel Jamison rode out together for a head-count on their father's cattle, four miles south-southeast of Tularosa, that late afternoon. Both teenage brothers carried rifles for their own defense, and both were lately fired when searchers found their ravaged corpses close to sundown, on the range, together with Bent's mutilated gelding. Cabel's mount had made it home riderless, to signal the emergency.

Again, no suspects, and the district had run short of feral dogs to execute. Authorities, such as they were, professed their total bafflement. A cougar, possibly, they said, or could it be a grizzly bear? Tracks at the scene, as usual, were too ambiguous to say with any certainty.

September and October faded into history, all doors and windows locked in Tularosa after sundown, and particularly on outlying farms. The full moon pattern was observed, but no one dared to trust the other nights in any given month, without a warrant of the slayer's constancy. It, he or they struck randomly, without regard to compass points or choice of victims, whether lone or in small groups, at home or in the fields.

No one was safe.

Monday, November twenty-third, was stark and cold, but dry. No snow had fallen yet, but locals smelled it on the wind and knew it wouldn't be much longer till white blankets lay over their homes and lands. As if anticipating winter and its known restrictions on perambulation, came the killer one more time before year's end. The strike, at Nasker's Hardware Store inside the village, claimed Steve Nasker, the proprietor, his wife Helene, daughter Christine, turned ten the week before, and three-year-old son David.

Neighbors who revealed the carnage after sunup granted that they'd heard screaming around midnight, with the attendant sounds of struggle, but had been afraid to intervene. They blamed the village marshal for his failure to maintain patrols, while he advanced bronchitis and incipient pneumonia in his own defense.

The interesting part, if such it could be called: some of the blood discovered at the latest scene appeared to be the killer's, spilled when Helene Nasker slashed him with a scythe they had on sale, after the district's recent harvest. Conversation with the village doctor and a survey of the neighborhood revealed no one with any recent wounds to match the bloodstained tool.

Winter passed in shades of gray and brown, as usual. Through December, January, February, no more homicides occurred in Tularosa or environs. No relief came with cessation of the crimes this time, only an anxious waiting for spring's advent and the startup of another hunting season. In the past, that meant mule dear and pronghorn antelope, perhaps the odd black bear. In 1875 humans were on the list.

Specifically, on Monday night, March twenty-ninth, it was a deputy hired on by Tularosa's marshal, doubling his power to surveil the village. Myron Decker was a twenty-year-old part-time handyman, fairly adept at carpentry, less so with the Colt Model 1861 Navy revolver his employer had provided for his rounds of Tularosa. On the night he died, Decker had drawn the pistol but forgot to cock it when he was attacked, under a bright full moon. He fought back with it anyway, to no effect, and when a tradesman found his body in the morning, Myron lacked a head, one arm, and sundry vitals. Tularosa's barber found the head behind his shop; the arm turned up at Tularosa's Free Will

Baptist Church, an altar offering; and Decker's missing organs spent the next two days appearing in assorted corners of the village.

That was it, so far—or, rather, Thorn had managed to collect no more reports of local slayings on his recent travels back and forth across the U.S. border into Mexico. Nor had capture of a suspect, bound to be reported in the largest type available for headlines, been announced since Myron Decker met his grisly end.

So Thorn was coming now to have a closer look-see for himself.

He rode a tall gray stallion he called Shadow, sired by proud Arabians spanning some four millennia. Shadow had chosen Thorn, as much as he chose it, silent communication shared between them and the stallion's acquiescence to a stranger, where its other would-be riders wound up groveling in dust. His second animal, a molly pack mule he called Bell for no apparent reason, bore the trappings of his rootless lifestyle on the trail: bedroll; cooking utensils; food and drink; spare ammunition; basic tools for shoeing horse and mule; a change of clothing (black); and Thorn's accumulated files, contained in envelopes labeled by state, within a stout valise.

A talent from Thorn's childhood, never mentioned to acquaintances of any stripe, was his capacity for opening mental communication with most animals. It failed him in the world of insects, but beyond that—growing stronger up the evolutionary chain from fish to reptiles and amphibians, then birds and mammals—he had learned to carry on what passed for silent conversation in some cases, steer specific creatures to his will, and stave off the occasional attack by roaming predators at large. There was no magic to it, in Thorn's mind, although he did not fully understand the knack himself. It simply *was,* a talent born in him and honed over the years by Aunt Drusilla, constantly pursuing means of contact with the Other Side of varied planes. A generation earlier, some rural townies might have strung him up for witchcraft, if they could have caught and held him. Some still might attempt it if he flaunted his peculiar gift, so Thorn refrained from sharing it with human beings whom, in many cases, he regarded as a lower form of life.

With them, allegedly *his* kind, communication fell back onto spoken words, and even those were frequently inadequate.

Shadow required only the subtlest urging to maintain his course toward Tularosa now, and Bell followed from habit, trudging out the hours of their days, anticipating rest stops and their nightly campouts as an end to labor for the moment. Thorn made certain not to burden her unduly and to always thank the mule for serving him, performing tasks he could not do alone.

Camping this Thursday evening at dusk—coincidentally, one night before the territory's next full moon—Gideon Thorn already knew what to expect in Tularosa. Locals would regard him, rightly, as a stranger and outsider. They'd resent him opening old wounds, picking at scabs they wished would heal, soliciting whatever details that the press had failed to spill about their local crimes and losses. He would not approach survivors of the victims first, a self-defeating exercise, but would attempt the public and official route. The marshal was a prime source, likewise any gatherers of gossip, like the barber, minister, and so on. Where a scene remained for visiting, he'd view it.

Somewhere in the midst of that research, with any luck, the slayer might find him.

In that event, Gideon Thorn reckoned he was prepared —or, at the very least, as much as he could be.

Sleeping that night beneath Otero County's stars, Shadow and Molly tethered near him with a fair amount of grass and water burbling from a little stream he'd found, Thorn had no fear of being taken by surprise. No one knew he was on his way to Tularosa—not unless, perhaps, the killer he'd come hunting was an animal in fact—and while the district harbored human border trash, flotsam from Reconstruction-era Texas and continual upheavals going on in Mexico—Thorn lost no sleep to fear of human predators obstructing him. Such incidents had happened twice so far, outside of Amarillo and in El Paso del Norte, across the border from El Paso, Texas, neither of them ending well for Thorn's assailants.

He had no opinion, much less moral standards, when it came to spilling human blood. If violence was unavoidable, Thorn meant to strike first and eliminate the threat as rapidly as possible. People, unlike most animals, had choices. They did not react from pure instinct, but often from the faults of greed, jealousy, rage, and superstition.

Only on the last point did the standard blur for Thorn. What many saw as childish nonsense, Thorn regarded as a tuning in, perhaps imperfect and misunderstood, to Something Else, beyond the normal sphere of human senses, like his own mental discourse with animals. Some people, evidence had taught him, served as portals to the Other Side.

And some, of course, were simply lunatics.

Tomorrow night was Tularosa's next full moon, and he would be there to observe it. After two months of inaction, he could not predict whether the phantom killer would return to claim more victims or continue his hiatus, biding time. In either case, Gideon Thorn had come prepared to linger for the time required to satisfy himself that something supernatural either had happened in the village, or had not. If not, he would attempt to learn the killer's name and give it up before he moved on, disappointed yet again, continuing the search for whatever he sought.

A monster, certainly, though last glimpsed for a moment only, twenty-one years earlier and some four hundred forty miles away. Few normal creatures in the wild survived that long or roamed that far. As for *abnormal* creatures. well...

Gideon Thorn would have to wait and see.

TWO

The African arrived by coach and caused a nine-day's wonder among staff members at Bledsoe's Home for Orphaned Boys. He had begun his westward journey via train from Boston to Chicago, then Rock Island, Illinois, where track ran out. A ferry trundled him across the Mississippi River, armed with freedom papers duly notarized and witnessed by two U.S. congressmen, as he pressed on by road through Iowa, crossed the southeastern corner of Nebraska, and proceeded into Bleeding Kansas, where the scourge of slavery was yet to be decided by a referendum of the territory's white male voters. In the given atmosphere, the traveler carried two pistols and a curved Mangbetu knife, used as a form of currency in Africa but equally suited to self-defense.

His name—Obi Magoro—was unknown in Kansas, his appearance no less strange to Anglo-European eyes. He wore a broadcloth morning suit, three-piece, surmounted by a black felt bowler hat, with lace-up ankle boots. His walking stick was ebony, crowned with a silver lion's snarling head, and it concealed a rapier's blade for those occasions when his other weapons might not be available. In fact, until he reached Bledsoe's in Lawrence, none of the assorted arms were necessary.

Armand Bledsoe, founder and proprietor of the repository for unwanted boys, initially regarded his dark visitor with arch disdain. That attitude began to dissipate as he perused the documents Magoro carried, not only identifying him as a free man, but naming his employer as Drusilla Agnes Thorn, a stalwart member of Old Boston's Brahmin class who bought and sold the likes of Bledsoe for what they considered pocket change. He still might have objected, but the letter signed by Henry Gardner, Governor of Massachusetts, broke him with its urging in the strongest terms that he cooperate, implying a review of Bledsoe's license by the Kansas territorial authorities if he refused.

With that in mind, Bledsoe summoned Gideon Thorn, survivor of a tragic incident in western Kansas Territory and, as he now learned, Drusilla Thorn's only surviving relative. The lad would be returning with her trusted aid, Obi Magoro, to the dwindling family's manse on Boston's Beacon Hill. Magoro had a twenty-dollar bill for Bledsoe, in exchange for which Bledsoe would write, and his attorney would immediately notarize, a letter detailing the purpose of a white child's traveling together with a black man from the territory back to Massachusetts. Any failure of said letter to appease police or others in the Kansas Territory would be deemed Bledsoe's responsibility.

Gideon Thorn, still shy of three years old, was dazzled by his first encounter with Obi Magoro. He would never fully lose that sense of wonder in Magoro's presence, though with time and interaction he would come to view the African as a devoted friend. Only the terms of Aunt Drusilla's will and the advance of Obi's age—albeit at a seeming snail's pace—had prevented him from joining Thorn on his perambulation of the West in recent months.

At first, though, they were still learning to know each other, from the introduction awkwardly performed by Armand Bledsoe to Magoro telling Gideon that he possessed an aunt of whom he'd never heard before. Not only was she living, and in far-off Boston, but she was *extremely* wealthy, on the scale of Vanderbilts and Astors, two more families of whom young Gideon possessed no information whatsoever. He'd believed he was a castaway, a cipher. Now, learning that he had family and they were rich, he boggled at the thought, like something from a fairy tale.

Obi Magoro startled Thorn once more by speaking perfect English, addressing him as "Master Gideon," although without the slightest intimation of servility. When he suggested that Thorn pack his things, it clearly was an order, one that Gideon was happy to obey. In truth, he had few things to pack, and nothing but a paper bag to hold them: the pajamas he'd been found in, on the verge of frostbite, in November; one spare shirt; a toothbrush; and a comb with which he tried in vain to hide the white streak running through his coal-black hair from front to back. Magoro viewed the bag's contents, deposited them in a leather satchel, and informed Gideon that they would buy more fitting items on their journey eastward.

Thus, without a good-by or a backward glance, began Gideon's journey to the East, reversing Obi's course from Lawrence back to Clifton, Iowa, beside the Mississippi River via coach; crossing the broad water by boat to reach Rock

Island, and embarking on the first of several trains that carried them, in time, to the Boston and Lowell Railroad's station in Massachusetts. There, a carriage waited for them, driven by a long-faced white man in a cape and top hat, who addressed Magoro as "milord" and stowed their luggage for the thirty-mile last leg from Lowell to Beacon Hill.

At Gideon's first glimpse of Aunt Drusilla's home—her *mansion*—he immediately knew there must be some mistake. Why would his parents live and die in a small cabin on the east slope of the Rockies, when they could have shared such splendor and a life of luxury? Convinced that there had been some grievous error, probably a mix-up of his name with someone else's, Gideon stood silently beside the coach, his satchel dragging down one shoulder, waiting for the axe to fall.

And then his aunt emerged, flanked by a pair of servants in their livery. She scrutinized him carefully, not seeming thrilled by what she saw, then moved to stand before him, bending down to take his hand in hers and pump it twice. Her gray eyes found their mirror image in his own and locked there.

"I am pleased to meet you, Nephew," she declared. "Now come. We have much work to do."

BOSTON: 1855-1869

And so they did. The lessons never ended; rather they grew more protracted and intense with time, but Gideon did not object. He realized that he had much to learn, not only about fitting in with what Bostonians regarded as "polite society"—a species altogether different from those found in New York, in Philadelphia, or, gods be praised, Chicago, that dissolute "Gem of the Prairie"—but also about getting by in life. There was a world beyond the city, he already knew, and someday he would visit it again.

For answers. For revenge.

Gideon's lessons started slowly, Aunt Drusilla aided by Obi Magoro, by her servants, and a governess employed to tutor Gideon before he reached the age for private school. The public schools in Boston had been organized two centuries before, but Aunt Drusilla did not trust them to prepare a candidate for Harvard University, her father's and grandfather's alma mater. Prior to entering a classroom of the school she had in mind for Gideon, he had to learn the finer points of manners, dress and grooming, and the rudiments of education that included reading, writing, and arithmetic.

He was presented to Society by slow degrees, at house and garden parties Aunt Drusilla staged for just that purpose, doling out slim details of his parents' death while "on an expedition" to the West. Since Gideon remembered little of The Incident—and shared far less, years later, to Obi Magoro—tamping down the lid on details was no problem. He was silent both by inclination and by training under Aunt Drusilla's roof.

And Gideon was equally reserved about his aunt's preoccupation with the Other Side, although she made no secret of that fascination with her private inner circle. She attended séances, consulted mediums, experimented with a ouija board imported from the Far East, practiced endlessly with tarot cards—a Colleoni-Baglioni deck—and delved deeply into all aspects of Spiritualism. In the latter pursuit, she hosted New York's three Fox sisters and Dr.

Paschal Beverly Randolph at her manse on Beacon Hill, picking their brains while they, even by Gideon's perception, tried to pick her pocket.

Aunt Drusilla had a knack for taking what she needed from a wide variety of sources and applying it to her own quest for knowledge, without falling into slavish thrall of seers and gurus on the rise. She bankrolled no one, published nothing on her own account, preferred to watch and listen rather than pontificate. Gideon, learning quickly, caught up with his aunt and then kept pace with her. Along the way, they both discovered his facility for animal communication and the fact that he possessed a photographic memory, both traits that Aunt Drusilla urged her ward to keep as closely guarded secrets.

In his sixth year, the fourth in Boston, Gideon enrolled as a first-grader at the Weatherford Academy and instantly collided with a wall of vintage snobbery. Most of his classmates knew each other from the cradle up, as playmates on their parents' walled estates and at their country homes. They spoke in childish shorthand about sporting and financial matters that were wholly new to Gideon, or barely understood. As usual in a society of boys who follow the example of their fathers, uncles, older brothers, there was hazing to endure, some of it verging upon brutality.

The first time Gideon came home with a black eye, his aunt considered storming off to see the headmaster, then took a breath and thought again. Instead of stepping in to fight Gideon's battle for him, she called on Obi Magoro to provide instruction in the manly art of self-defense.

Few residents of Boston were as suited to a given task. In Africa, before his transit Stateside as a servant, Obi had mastered Damble bare-knuckle boxing, Engolo ritual combat, and Nguni stick-fighting. Those martial arts conferred no colored belts, as in the Eastern styles, but each in turn required the same fitness, determination, and long practice to succeed. In lethal situations, any one of them could kill or cripple an opponent, although schoolyard rivalry demanded more restraint—another trait Gideon learned at Obi's hand.

During their practice sessions, he also observed the tribal scarring on Magoro's chest and shoulders, normally concealed by clothing. Gideon imagined how it must have felt to pass that test of manhood and decided being cuffed or body-slammed in training ranked as nothing by comparison.

Soon after Easter break in second grade he had the opportunity to use what he had learned against a pair of fifth-grade boys who thought "the orphan runt" an easy target for their malice. Specifically, one was a banker's son; the other was the youngest offspring of a lawyer on retainer from the Cabot family, renowned in shipping. After Gideon reduced them both to blood and tears, he brought a scathing letter home to Aunt Drusilla, threatening expulsion if he did not mend his ways and learn comportment of the form expected from a Weatherford enrollee.

That time, Aunt Drusilla *did* visit the headmaster. Gideon was not present for their closed-door meeting, but when she emerged, he glimpsed the educator's pallid face and caught that worthy blotting at his forehead with a handkerchief. There were no further difficulties during Gideon's tenure at Weatherford, and as he later understood, the flow of his aunt's generous donations to the school continued unabated, although teetering along a razor's edge.

Without the ongoing distraction of harassment, Gideon excelled in all his studies and at sports, where practice with

Obi Magoro honed his growing body into a well-oiled machine. He was strong at football, with its introduction during 1862, and better still at baseball, traveling several times with Obi Magoro to watch the Brooklyn Atlantics and New York Knickerbockers, until their league banned participation by blacks in 1867. In track and field, his true métier, Gideon played a solitary hand, taking medals in the long and broad jumps, pole vault, javelin, shot put, and hammer throw.

A warrior in the making, though he didn't know it yet.

And in his spare time, what there was of it, he thought about his parents, about brother Tommy, and the monster that had slain them, leaving him to bear its mark.

HARVARD UNIVERSITY: 1869-1873

Gideon's entry into Harvard was expected, a foregone conclusion. In the worst scenario, he would have been accepted as a "legacy," based on his family's connection and continuing donations to the school, but his outstanding academic record obviated any need for such administrative subterfuge. He joined the Class of '73 as a freshman, plunged headlong into classes, and still found time to join the baseball, football, and the rowing teams.

Gideon's major may have seemed disjointed, but it steered him toward a bachelor's degree in liberal arts, the only imprimatur required for admission to Harvard's Law School. His courses included archaeology and anthropology; biology, botany, and zoology; classical literature; comparative religions and theology; history of both the world and the United States; psychology and sociology. His straight-A average entitled Gideon to graduate *summa cum laude* in May 1873, and while he accepted that honor, along with its gold tassel cord, he declined to speak as class vale-dictorian, claiming stage fright against the persistent urging of his faculty counselor.

In fact, he simply had so sage advice to offer any of his fellow graduates.

His mind was focused elsewhere, and while Gideon fully intended to proceed with plans for law school, he had grown increasingly determined that his future lay to west-ward. With a law degree he could go anywhere and set up shop, including Colorado, now a territory of its own, no longer part of Kansas, which had made the leap to state-hood back in January 1861. Twenty-nine months later—eight years after Gideon departed from the orphanage with Obi Magoro—William Quantrill's raiders sacked Lawrence, burning all but two of its businesses, killing some two hundred men and boys. Gideon sometimes wondered whether Armand Bledsoe was among the dead or if he'd managed to escape, but in the end it made no difference.

Before he started law school in the fall of 1873, Gideon determined to take the summer off and tour Europe. Aunt Drusilla cheerfully concurred, and dropped her first sugges-tion that Obi Magoro tag along with him when Gideon insisted it was time to try something himself, without a guiding hand. What could go wrong in London, Paris, Rome, Vienna, or Berlin?

In fact, nothing went wrong on his end of the trip, which was meticulously planned and bankrolled by his Aunt Drusilla—no objection there, since Gideon would not gain access to his trust fund until he had graduated with his Juris Doctor and had passed the Massachusetts bar exam. Gideon spent a week in London, another in Paris, and had barely set foot in Vienna when the news reached him from home, delivered by a concierge at the Hotel Imperial. A lawyer he had never met wrote Gideon from Boston, saying Aunt Drusilla had collapsed during a visit to the Globe Theater on July 2, passing from the stroke that took her down near dawn of the following day.

Disconsolate, Gideon sailed as soon as it was feasible, from La Rochelle in France after a harried train ride westward across the Austrian Empire and on through Switzerland. The ship's crossing took nine days, forcing Gideon to miss the Drusilla's funeral at Forest Hills Cemetery, but he made that his second stop, after checking in on Beacon Hill with Obi Magoro. The mausoleum in which she lay with seven generations of her ancestors was large enough to house a family, its sculpted stone exterior festooned with lichen, ivy climbing to the eaves. Gideon went inside but didn't like the pent-up air and soon left, never to return.

He feared Magoro might be dispossessed somehow, but Aunt Drusilla had provided for him in her will. With no surviving relatives but Gideon to claim a share of her estate, she left the manse to him on the condition that Magoro must remain until his death or choice to leave, whichever happened first. If he departed voluntarily, Obi would take one million dollars with him, to dispense as he saw fit, but had no further claim on the estate.

As for the rest, it now belonged to Gideon, with oversight from the respected Brahmin legal firm of Messrs. Block, Enright and Sloan. The partners had administered the Thorn family's finances since 1821, with sons succeeding fathers at the office, and had earned Drusilla's trust during the depression of 1839 to '43, keeping the family's fortune intact while others foundered and sank.

One alteration in Drusilla's will exempted Gideon from

going on to law school if he felt a different calling. She already knew his mind, bolstered by private conversations with Magoro, and her own preoccupation with the paranormal—not to mention brother Aaron's death, poorly investigated at the time and still unsolved in Aunt Drusilla's mind—compelled her to support Gideon's urge to travel west, examine details of his family's massacre if that were possible, and seek to learn the truth. When he began collecting news cuttings on other outré cases from beyond the Mississippi River she did not object, but rather helped him with additions of her own as they became available from magazines and papers she subscribed to.

Beyond that point it was a relatively simple matter of equipage, plotting routes, and getting on the move. Gideon had no ties to sever in the city or at school, and would not say good-by to Obi when he planned for them to meet again. If something intervened beforehand and their parting was the last time they would ever speak, who better to process and deal with that end than Magoro?

In the meantime, half a continent lay waiting for Gideon Thorn.

So many strange reports, so little time.

THREE

Gideon Thorn rose with the sun and got an early start, his last day on the trail. He could have ridden into Tularosa after nightfall, but he's chosen not to make his first approach in darkness, with the village already on edge and no one physically available for questioning. He'd have a hard enough time getting by in daylight, without spooking locals in the dark and getting shot by accident.

The village wasn't much to look at, riding in. Only established twelve years earlier, it hadn't spread out much from its original forty-nine parcels of land, mapped and duly recorded. The town's *acequia*—a community-run watercourse used in Spain and its former Western colonies for irrigation—gave the village a unique appearance, trees and private gardens lining the streets, but its houses were basic adobe with roofs made of tin, tiles, or thatch. Downtown, if you could call it that, the lone hotel was made of wood, as were the few shops flanking it: the barber's place, a feed store, Nasker's former hardware shop, a legal office, and the marshal's jail. Adobe had been good enough for a saloon-cum-restaurant, the misnamed Lucky Strike, and for the village's two churches, Catholic and Free Will Baptist, one at either end of town.

The good news was its livery, a spacious barn erected on the southern end of town, as if expecting visitors who hadn't yet arrived. When Thorn checked in, the hostler, fifty-something with a long but well-combed beard, saw to his stallion and the mule as if they'd come in with a royal carriage, promising that they'd be ready day or night, as Gideon required.

Leaving his basic gear, hauling his guns, Thorn moved along to the hotel, which styled itself the Tularosa House. Not grandiose, but still a bit pretentious when he tried it on his tongue. The check-in clerk blinked once to see a stranger walking in, so obviously armed for bear or something larger, but a smile broke out between his mustache and goatee as he remembered he was there to serve the public, not to judge them.

"Yes, sir! May I help you?"

Gideon stated the obvious, his quest to find a room. The place had ten, with one of those already occupied, so he was free to choose and picked one on the second floor, facing across toward the saloon. Why not? It might be noisier at night than sleeping toward the back, but anything he saw and learned about the town might benefit him later.

When a dollar had changed hands and he'd received his key, Thorn went upstairs and found his room sufficient, if a comedown from the lodgings he would have expected in a larger town. It had the basics, though: a brass bed with its mattress barely sagging; dresser with its mirror still intact; a chamber pot he might use and a brass spittoon he never would. The closet was an alcove large enough to hold his saddlebags and second suit. There was a privy in the fenced-off rear. A public bath, as he'd already seen, was operated by the barber, two doors down.

Back on the street, he turned that way, deciding that his next stop ought to make him more presentable From there, he'd go back to the Lucky Strike and see what they were offering for lunch, before he started making rounds and rubbing locals the wrong way.

There was no question they'd resent him. Thorn could only wait and see how much.

The barber, curiously, was a bald man, but he sported muttonchops and a luxuriant mustache to make up for his shiny pate. At sight of Thorn he beamed and said, "Good morning, stranger! Ace Donovan, barber and sole proprietor of Tularosa Baths."

"Gideon Thorn." He couldn't help but ask: "Your parents called you 'Ace'?"

"They called me Arthur. 'Ace' comes from a lucky poker hand, a long time back."

"Well, Ace, I need a bath, as you can see, together with a haircut and a shave."

"You've come to the right place, sir. Any preference as to the order?"

"Bath first, if it's not a problem."

"Not at all. This way, please."

Thorn followed the barber through a curtained doorway to a backroom where two copper tubs stood on claw-footed legs, making the place's plural name correct. Neither was filled, but pots of water rested on a nearby stove, steaming away.

"If I could give your duds a brush while you're reclining, sir?"

29

"Sounds good," Thorn said, undressing without any false embarrassment after he'd placed his gunbelt on a chair beside the right-hand tub. His hat went on a wall peg, boots standing beneath it, but the weapons would stay close to hand.

"Those pendants are unique, if I may say so," Donovan remarked, as he began to fill the tub with water that looked piping hot.

Thorn idly thumbed the cluster of religious symbols hanging from a silver chain around his neck. Included, all crafted in silver, were a cross, a Star of David, crescent moon of Islam, and a pentagram for pagans. "I collect them in my travels," he replied.

"I lean toward shaving mugs myself, not that I travel much these days," Donovan said.

Testing the water with a foot, Gideon found it bearable and slipped into the tub, confirming that his Colts and Bowie knife were all within his easy reach. The barber left him with a bar of homemade soap and brace of fluffy towels before retreating with Thorn's suit.

Gideon soaked a while, then soaped himself as best he could within the confines of the tub, and he had stepped out onto tile, was drying off when Donovan returned with his refurbished clothes. After he'd dressed, Gideon joined the barber in his shop and took the only chair, hands near his guns as he was draped and treated to a warm towel covering his face. He asked no questions until Donovan was lathering his face in preparation for his shave.

"I hear you've had some tragedies around the village," Thorn remarked.

The barber stropped his razor. Said, "I reckon they've been newsworthy, yes sir."

"Still no solution, last I heard."

The razor slid across one cheek and followed Thorn's jawline. "None yet, sir. It's a bafflement, I grant you."

"Always falling on the night of a full moon, but not consistently."

"No sir." Donovan's blade followed the long curve of his neck. "That has been puzzling the law and all of us."

"Speaking of law," said Gideon, "what is your local marshal's name, again?"

Donovan wiped his razor on a towel and started on the other side. "Heck Halliday. You might've seen his office yonder."

"Yet another name I doubt his parents had in mind at birth."

"I couldn't answer as to that," the barber said. "You'd have to ask the man himself."

Thorn shifted once again, keeping jaw movements to a minimum as Donovan began shaving his other side. "What's your opinion of the murders, Ace?"

"I couldn't rightly say. At first, we all thought it was animals, of course. But later on, after it busted into Nasker's place and killed that family...it *has* to be a man, wouldn't you say?"

"That's what I'm hoping to discover."

"You, sir? Do you represent the law?"

"Simply an interested passerby," Thorn said, "with insight into certain cases such as this."

The barber cleaned his razor prior to putting it away, and patted Thorn's cheeks with witch hazel. "Cases such as this, you say? There's more around?"

"No two identical, of course. But still...indicative."

Donovan started on Thorn's hair, making no comment on its slash of white. His effort was more of a trim than anything, rounding the hair that brushed Thorn's shirt collar, tidying around his ears. After a momentary lapse he asked, "This keeps you busy, does it, sir?"

"More than a pastime," Gideon replied. "It's my vocation."

"And it pays well, if I may ask?"

"Not a dime so far, alas."

"But, then..."

"My curiosity appears to be insatiable."

"In that case, sir, I wish you all good fortune." Donovan applied a whiskbroom, dusted Thorn with talcum powder, and removed the drape. "Ready to face the world."

Paying his tab, Gideon answered back, "But is it ready to face me?"

Leaving the shop, Gideon thought he'd sown enough questions and hints to start the village buzzing. Barbers, in his personal experience, ranked high among the gossip vendors in most towns, and he had no doubt that Ace Donovan would spread the substance of their conversation, possibly with personal embellishments along the way. That suited Thorn as he moved toward the Lucky Strike, to satisfy his hunger from the trail.

The tavern had a window facing on the street and smoky lanterns spaced around its walls. The waitress who approached him first and led him to a corner table was Hispanic, early twenties, dressed in a white ruffled blouse, a green full skirt, and sash of many colors tied around her narrow waist. She handed him a cardboard menu, worn from handling, and waited while he chose one of the combination plates—a steak with enchiladas, rice and beans—together with a beer to wash it down.

Chips came ahead of anything, with fresh-made

guacamole. Gideon had barely started on it when the door swung open, spilling sunlight on the floor. A solitary figure scanned the room, seeming to count its scattered customers, then homed in on Thorn's table. Gideon was not surprised to see he wore a badge, and gave the barber credit for the speed of his report.

So it begins, he thought.

"Heck Halliday," the new arrival said. "And you are...?"

"Having lunch."

"You take my meaning."

"Will you sit, Marshal? I plan on eating, and if you remain standing I'll have no choice but to avoid your eyes."

Reluctantly, it seemed, the lawman sat across from him, arms folded. "So," he said. "Your name?"

"Did Mr. Donovan neglect to tell you?"

While the marshal thought of how to answer that, Thorn's meal arrived with silverware.

"Something for you, Marshal?" the waitress asked.

"Just talk."

The meal she set before Gideon looked and smelled delicious. Before starting in on it, he said, "Gideon Thorn. Next question?"

Halliday *harrumphed,* then asked him, "What's your interest in our local situation, Mr. Thorn?"

"What situation would that be, Marshal?"

"I think you know."

"The murders."

"In a word, yes."

"I consider that a personal affair."

"Not when you're prying into others' and the business of the law."

"You have a point," he said, around a bite of beef and beans. "When I was young, my parents and my elder brother died in Kansas Territory. Savaged by an animal, the locals said. My memories of the event are vague and fragmentary but I question the official verdict. Now that I have time and resources to spare, I'm seeking answers from whatever venue may present itself."

Halliday frowned. "How long ago was this attack upon your family?"

"Twenty-one years."

"In Kansas Territory."

"Colorado, now."

"And you believe there's some connection between that and what's been happening in Tularosa?"

"That's *my* question, Marshal. So far, all I know is what I've read in newspapers."

"We covered all that ground, me and the county sheriff."

"And your files? Are they available for public scrutiny?"

"Authorized personnel."

"Who authorizes them?"

"That would be me."

"And what's your inclination, Marshal?"

Halliday frowned back at him. "If you were an official of some kind—"

"In any case."

"I'll have to think about it, Mr. Thorn."

"Of course. I'll leave you to it, then."

Taking his cue, Halliday rose. "I'd hate to see you rile the families," he said.

"Meaning survivors."

"Or their neighbors. Anyone at all, in fact."

"I don't make empty promises," Thorn said. "But I shall do my best."

"Or face the consequences."

"Threats already, Marshal?"

"Just a cautionary warning, Mr. Thorn."

Alone once more, Gideon sipped his beer and smiled. He counted the exchange as progress, knew the word would spread, between the barber and the marshal, maybe bringing others to him, or perhaps softening them for his approach. He planned to take it easy, the remainder of his first day in the village, waiting to find out what night and the full moon might bring.

There lay another risk, he realized. If something happened overnight, the marshal might try blaming Gideon for the coincidence of his arrival, but it wouldn't stick. He had been far away on all the other nights of carnage, nothing whatsoever to connect him with the other crimes. An alternate scenario, he thought, was that another killing might prompt Halliday to open up his files, however grudgingly, hoping fresh eyes might make a difference. In that event...

Thorn stopped himself. He hated wishing for another death by violence of strangers he had never met. It made him something of a vulture, in his own mind, but what other choices did he have? The Tularosa murders were irregular, despite their lunar cycle, skipping months at random. Try as he might, Thorn could not explain the secret of their lapses any more than he could pick the killer's name out of a hat.

There had to be a reason for the murders starting when they did, perhaps a new arrival in the neighborhood before the first two deaths, in February of last year. That was a question he could answer through land records, sales and purchases, without the marshal's help. A doctor and/or undertaker would be useful, too, together with the minister whose church had been defiled.

Witnesses of a sort, though none had seen the killer personally.

Or had they?

In a town so small Gideon thought the killer *must* be known to someone, though the holders of that knowledge might not realize his guilt. There might be signs the locals overlooked, through simple ignorance or disbelief that any friend of theirs could be responsible. Until Thorn knew what he was looking for, possessed a better grasp of all the facts, his speculation was in vain.

Gideon cleaned his plate, finished his beer, and left his payment on the table, with a fair tip for the waitress. The meal's size would allow him to skip dinner and return for breakfast. In the meantime, he was growing tired and headed back to his room at the Tularosa House, daylight still beaming down.

Upstairs, he double-locked the door, wedged his lone chair beneath its knob and drew the blinds, then stripped and hung his suit up in the closet. Standing at the mirror, Thorn examined his reflection with a focus on the small medallions worn around his neck. He hadn't managed to collect symbols for Buddhism or Hinduism yet, could not have said exactly what they were, but those he wore felt adequate for now.

Gideon had no personal conviction to one faith over another. He believed that all caught glimpses of the Other Side, but none had grasped it clearly, all being preoccupied on earthly planes with money and control. The pinnacle of power for a "holy" man was his ability to charm and wield authority over a flock, dictating what they did and thought, their sex lives and child-rearing, their pursuit of ultimate "salvation" at the end of life. Many whom he had met were simply charlatans; others impressed him as sincere, although a lunatic could pass the same broad test.

Gideon Thorne *believed,* after his years with Aunt Drusilla and his long talks with Obi Magoro, but he wasn't sure on any given day *what* he believed. He was convinced that something lingered on the Other Side, but whether it was ascertainable, if it concerned itself with humans on a steady basis, he remained unsure.

As for his own case and the job at hand...well, who could say? Was there a link between the murders, more than twenty years apart? Were Tularosa's homicides the work of animals, one person, or a gang?

Thorn took his Winchester and gunbelt with him into bed, wanting the weapons close by as he slept. Any intruders would make noise enough to rouse him and receive a heated welcome on the threshold, even if they caught him dozing in the nude. Whatever came of that, if it occurred, would be between him and Heck Halliday.

Sleep rarely troubled Thorn. The single chilling nightmare from his childhood came but rarely now, after two decades, and on those occasions he observed the incident almost as an outsider, watching from an elevated distance, straining for more details in the murk of swirling snow and darkness, riven by his mother's screams. He never felt the pain of being slashed across his scalp but watched it happen, saw the spurt of blood along the line that would be snow-white later on.

Thorn slept, but woke near midnight, shifting in his bed. Around the blinds he'd drawn, pale moonlight slipped into the room. If anything happened this night, he thought, it was already underway, and there was nothing he could do about it now.

Nothing but wait and see what morning brought: a

ghastly revelation or another full-moon night passed by with nothing to report. The first might put him on a fresh scent, while the other simply meant that he was wasting time.

Resting a hand atop one of his Colts, Gideon Thorn went back to sleep.

FOUR

SOUTHWEST OF TULAROSA: JUNE 18, 1875

The predator feels strong, invigorated, powerful. Walking by moonlight always makes it feel this way, as if an energy from Heaven has infected it, swelling its muscles, making every fiber of its being yearn for action. It can smell the night, a thousand scents demanding full attention, from the tang of sagebrush to the dread sweat of a rabbit in its lair.

The rabbit has nothing to fear, nor does the desert rat, the antelope, or any other beast that travels on four legs. Even the sheep it smells tonight—so many of them, fat and slow, their meat delicious when it's eaten raw—are safe, although their tiny brains cannot accept that thought. The predator wants only manflesh. Nothing else will serve to satisfy its hunger.

Thus it always is and has been for the night-prowler. It craves a certain meal and when deprived, as it has been the past three months, its craving turns inward, feeding upon its own flesh, muscles, and internal organs. It begins to wither, slowly, helpless, free to roam only on special nights and even then, sometimes constrained.

But when it's free to roam and hunt, then life is good.

The sheep are still a mile or more away, but it can smell them—and their watchers. Two humans tonight, related, but their scents are different for all of that, a fine distinction that the predator has learned to draw among the members of its prey group. Young or old, hygienic or contemptuous of soap and water, male or female, everything about a target serves in practice to set it apart and please the predator's senses.

Last time, its prey was middle-aged and tough, but had a taste of life about him for all that. The whiskey he enjoyed had soaked into the human's meat and given it an unexpected tang that made the predator a little giddy, reckless, on the verge of risking capture. Something in the man's scent had reminded it of liquor, tantalizing and repulsive at the same time, but it went ahead regardless.

Once the hunger grips it, there can be no turning back.

Three months without a decent feeding, two full moons gone by without a taste of bloody flesh, makes hunger sharp and desperate. Two targets mean a greater risk, but once the predator has locked onto them, it cannot resist. Only the last-minute appearance of an army—or the one call it cannot deny—will stay the prowler from its course.

And even that lone call, its Master's voice, is growing weaker. Long weeks in restraint have taught the predator to think about resistance, hoard its strength and make a stand against the solitary force that has restrained it up till now. Rebellion is a possibility that tantalizes and whose time, it feels convinced, is coming soon.

When it is truly free, at liberty to rule the night, who can foretell its final limits? Why should there be any in the world of darkness where it reigns? As for the daylight realm, it has already learned to play the game, conceal itself and watch its prey pass by, marking this one or that for lingering attention in the future.

It pauses now and sniffs the midnight air, snout raised, eyes fastened on the white orb of its Mother Moon above. The town, behind it and away to the northeast, gives off its usual aroma of congestion, people crammed together, living side by side. The desert wind ruffles its fur and seems to glide *beneath* it, stroking flesh and raising goose flesh.

Half a mile and closing now. One of the humans is asleep, the other sipping coffee on his watch over the sheep, fearful that coyotes or wolves will raid the flock. If he were more attuned to night and Nature, this man would be wary of the danger to himself.

Good for the predator that he is not. Instead, another stupid member of a moron race sits waiting for it, almost offering its life up as a sacrifice.

The predator is happy to accept.

It seems unjust that only one night in a given month releases it to feed, a question that has nagged the predator with no solution readily accessible. It mulls the problem during daylight hours, finds no answer, but a possibility suggests itself.

When it is strong enough at last to rid itself of bondage to the Master, might it then be free to hunt on any night it likes and sate itself at will? Perhaps it will escape the weeks of growing, gnawing hunger and begin to realize its full potential as the lord of all that it surveys.

A dream to cherish, but for tonight, its chosen targets are enough.

. . .

"Miguel! *Depsertarse!*" Eladio Cardenas said, half whispering, to rouse his son. He did not want his voice to carry any farther than the dim glow of their campfire, a poor imitation of the pallid moon.

Miguel woke grudgingly, as if aware his four hours of sleep had more than three hours to run. "*Qué pasa, papa?*" he questioned.

"Something's coming," said his father.

"What?"

"I don't know yet. Get up and arm yourself."

Once he received the order, Miguel did not hesitate. At thirteen years of age, he was already lithe and strong, pushing at manhood and inured to rigors of the outdoor life, tending their sheep and getting by on what was earned from wool or meat in any given year, he would replace Eladio someday—or not, as destiny decreed. Each man must find his own way in the world, and if Miguel did not wish to remain a shepherd, there was nothing that Eladio could do or say to hold him. His father, once a miner, had been forced to learn that lesson, as had *his* father, a soldier, years before.

The wheel of life turned constantly, grinding the slow and awkward into pulp beneath it, leaving others in its wake to wonder what went wrong. A few got out ahead, however briefly, and ran free until they were consumed in turn.

Miguel was on his feet and had his hat on, as if moonlight had the same impact as noon's relentless glare. The weapon he'd retrieved from underneath his blanket, never far away, was a single shot, muzzle-loading Springfield rifle musket used during the white men's War Between the States, chambered to fire a .58-caliber Minié ball. In practice, with no pressure on him, he could load and fire three rounds per minute, but at night and in the face of danger, it would likely be one shot or nothing.

Eladio was carrying a double-barreled coach gun made by Remington, ten-gauge, loaded with buckshot that would stop a wolf, coyote, fox, or man at twenty paces. Out beyond that range, he hoped the weapon's noise alone would be enough to do the trick and put an enemy to flight.

Or would it?

He was troubled by the full moon and by Tularosa's history. Cardenas and his son had not been present in Otero County last year, when the worst bloodletting happened, but they had been settled in the area by March and ghastly stories traveled quickly among people of all races. Everyone knew what had happened to the Anglos, on their farms and twice within the town itself, but what else could Cardenas do with sheep, except to graze and watch them as he'd learned when he was young and thought the world could still be his someday?

"I don't hear anything," Miguel said, moments later.

"Nor do I," his father answered back. "I *feel* it. That is something you must learn if you intend to make your way with animals." Wasted advice, perhaps, but he forged on. "Sheep don't announce their consternation, as with cows and horses. By the time they bleat and run, it is too late."

"Well, I am ready," said Miguel, "in any case." There was a skepticism in his voice, as if he thought his father might have been imagining the threat.

"Not yet," Eladio replied. "Your musket has a longer range but only one shot at a time. You wait here and listen. I shall go among the sheep and try to soothe them, hopefully confront whatever is disturbing them and kill it or persuade it to move on. If I should fail..."

He shrugged by failing firelight. There was nothing

more to say. If he went out to face the threat, whatever it might be, and proved unequal to the task, his son would have to carry on alone. Defend the flock, protect himself, and do whatever might be possible to salvage it tomorrow, when the sun rose.

Parting from the campfire's fading light and heat, Eladio wondered what form the peril to his flock would take this time. He knew the desert's predators, had also dealt with human rustlers in the past, and evil men who simply hated sheep and those who tended them. Tonight, though, it felt *different*, perhaps because of where he was.

And just possibly, he thought, because of the full moon.

The predator can see by moonlight as if it were day, high noon, with everything revealed. In fact, moonlight is *better* than the hot and unforgiving sun. It bathes the landscape with a mellow light but does not sear the skin or scorch the eyes.

The small campfire, still fifty yards away, glows hot, with red coals clustered at its core. A human figure passes back and forth before it, roaming, weak eyes scouring the darkness all in vain. A second, older human has advanced beyond the firelight, moving out amongst the sheep to settle them and find out what has roused some of the flock from drowsing in the dark. The herd is quiet, more or less, a mumble-muttering among some of the animals that has not risen to the bleating level yet, but once the killing starts the predator expects all that to change.

Chaos is part of the excitement, after all.

And from the humans, abject fear.

The predator approaches, circling warily, remaining downwind of the older man who guards the herd. It is unlikely that the human's senses have developed to the point of scenting danger on the wind, but why take chances? A surprise attack is preferable, neutralizing weapons, heightening the target's panic, ending with the sweet release of hot, fresh blood.

To that end, crouching as it moves among the sheep, the predator is conscious of a paradoxical desire. On the approach, it almost wishes there could be less moonlight beaming down, more shadows to conceal it, but an instant spasm of regret sends needling tremors through its tall, muscular frame. It *needs* the moonlight as a fish needs water, to exist. It will prevail in all its efforts, not *despite* the moon, but rather by absorbing and accepting its great power.

Sixty yards to contact with the prowling shepherd, and the predator can smell his weapon now, gun oil and steel, with a patina of the hunter's nervous sweat. The former makes it doubly cautious, while the latter makes the predator's mouth water.

At fifty yards the man is still traveling upwind with slow and measured steps. He whispers to the sheep in Spanish, tries to soothe them, and it seems to work a little, though their natural responses are attuned more finely to reality than any human's. Every member of the flock knows danger is approaching, while the man, despite his seeming prescience, still has a reserve of doubt.

Why else does he *approach* the threat, instead of fleeing for his miserable life?

At the fire, the man's assistant—no, his *offspring*—waits and watches nothing, finds no target for his rifle even in the bright moonlight. He's useless and will have that lesson driven home for the last time within a few more moments.

Neither of them is a match for the superior Nature has sent to slaughter them.

At thirty yards the predator drops to all fours, less comfortable than a crouch and lesser still than walking upright, but the skulking sheep provide its cover now. The shepherd is alert within his limits, weak eyes scanning for an enemy he senses but can't locate in time to save his life.

Clutching one of the sheep, the predator begins to guide it, steer it toward the flock's keeper. It is a bold ploy, but the animal it's chosen offers no protest. In fact, it almost seems relieved to have a guiding hand direct it, brushing off the burden of a personal decision: left or right, forward of back? Now it moves as directed by the predator and seems almost at peace.

The final rush surprises two of them, the sheep and shepherd. Charging with a snarl, the predator reaches its man while he is half turning to face it, leveling his gun. A flash of talons sends the double muzzles of his weapon angling skyward, pointed more or less toward Mother Moon as they discharge their wasted thunder. Teeth and claws rip into flesh and fabric. Slavering, the predator welcomes a heady rush of blood.

"Papa! *Lo que está sucediendo?*"

Miguel's father did not answer, but the boy knew what was happening—if not precisely, then at least in basic terms. He'd heard the double shotgun blast and seen the muzzle flashes pointed toward the dark sky, not a warning from his father, but a sign that some attacker had surprised him, prompting the discharge and leaving him effectively unarmed.

Whether he was alive or not, Miguel could not have said and was afraid to ask the night.

Defense came down to him now, covering the herd himself, and finding out what fate had claimed his father. If Eladio Cardenas was alive, he obviously needed help. So did the sheep, frightened and milling now, deciding in their odd way whether they should bolt as one or simply trot away in various directions and the herd be damned.

Miguel cocked his Springfield musket and slipped his index finger through the trigger guard, ready to fire. He'd have one chance and only one, before the midnight prowler either savaged him or fled, and neither was the outcome he desired. His father's failure to respond immediately told Miguel that Papa must be seriously injured, maybe dead or dying from the trauma his attacker had inflicted, and if he was still alive, the jolting burro ride to Tularosa—leaving all their sheep behind, there was no remedy for that— would likely finish him.

"No," Miguel muttered under his breath. "*Se termina aquí.*"

It ends here.

He would face whatever menaced him, his father, and their livelihood. His selfish dreams of running off to be a cowboy, maybe back at home in Mexico, would have to wait. He had responsibilities now thrust upon him, and a man did what he had to do.

Step one: move well out from the fire and cease appearing to the enemy in silhouette. He had to join the other side and take advantage of the night.

Step two: if he could spot a target in the moonlight, use the flip-up sights if feasible, aim low and *squeeze* the musket's trigger, careful not to jerk it back and spoil his single shot. If he should miss and be attacked, stand ready with the musket wielded as a fifty-six-inch club, smashing its nine pounds down onto his adversary's skull.

No man or animal could take that kind of punishment and live.

At least, no *mortal* man or animal.

But what if local rumors were correct, and they were dealing with a *cambiaformas,* a shapeshifter akin to the malicious *hombre-lobo*? How could anyone, much less a thirteen-year-old boy armed with a muzzle-loading weapon manufactured in the same year he was born, hope to slay a monster that defied human mortality?

"*Ridículo,*" he told himself, but could not wholly shake the superstition passed down through the generations of his people over centuries. Who was Miguel Cardenas to insist that all of them were wrong and he knew better at such tender age?

It hardly mattered now, in any case. Whatever might be hunting him after it took his father down, Miguel had lost his chance to flee. His only chance now was to stand and fight.

To be a man.

Brushing past sheep, he marveled at their evident stupidity. Even alarmed, they operated on a herd mentality, waiting for someone, anyone, to lead them out of danger. Driven by his own priority, to find his father first and then deal with the rest of it, Miguel pushed on, holding his weapon ready for the one shot that would either save or end his life.

He found his father moments later, sprawled on bloody earth, the fingers of his right hand still clutching the double-barreled scattergun. It had not saved him from the fangs and claws that ravaged him, shredding his throat and half his face, leaving his teeth and jaw bared through a flap of cheek, one eyeball dangling from its socket by a crimson thread. His chest was a deflated ruin under his tattered *camisa*, ribs showing, a loop of bowel extruded near the waistband of his trousers, where a rope served as his belt.

Stone dead, of course, but warm still, almost as if living, entrails steaming in the night.

Kneeling at his father's side, eyes blurred with tears, Miguel missed the first warning footsteps of his enemy. He turned too late, had the impression of a looming hairy shape, and by the time he raised the Springfield it was trapped beneath one arm, foreleg, whatever it might be, claws on the other ripping at his face.

And there was barely time to scream.

FIVE

TULAROSA; JUNE 19, 1875

Gideon Thorn was up and out to breakfast early, hiking from his hotel to the Lucky Strike. A different waitress greeted him and showed Thorn to a table near the combination bar and dining room's large window fronting what he guessed would be Main Street in any town that chose to name its thoroughfares. Another cardboard menu listed breakfast offerings, and Thorn chose ham with two fried eggs, a side of cubed potatoes cooked with onions, and a slab of toast with butter. Hot, black coffee topped it off.

While waiting for his meal, he watched the village come alive, foot traffic passing on the street, shopkeepers sweeping off their increments of wooden sidewalk, setting out displays they'd taken in at closing, sprucing up the items in their windows. Marshal Halliday passed down the street's far side, pausing to speak with merchants as he went, behaving like a politician on his rounds. One of the town's two preachers—had to be the Baptist, since he wore no backwards collar—crossed the street rather than share a sidewalk with the Lucky Strike.

Small towns, Thorn thought. They were as hidebound in their way as any clique at an exclusive school back East, or as the clubs rich elders formed to flaunt their wealth and influence before their peers. Boston was much the same, though on a grander scale, but larger cities offered more diversity, whole neighborhoods inhabited by immigrants whose language, customs and religion set them automatically at odds with others in the so-called "smelting pot" that was America.

In Tularosa, there was only one racial divide, between the Anglo-European crowd that ran the town and Mexicans. Chinese had not appeared in this part of the territory yet, while native Indians and certain transplants had been herded onto reservations deemed unfit for mining, cultivation, or for grazing herds. Whites cast a nervous eye across the border to their south, fearing incursion by the people whom they'd robbed of so much land during the ginned-up war of 1846 to '48.

Thorn's food came and he tucked into it avidly, impressed as on the day before by both the size and flavor of the serving. While he ate, he kept on watching people on the street, trying to guess their stories, read their faces, see which ones among them had been strained and frazzled by another full moon's passage overhead.

Living in fear was taxing. Knowing a certain date portended tragedy was worse, in Thorn's opinion, giving ample time to fret and brood, anticipating horror—and if, as on the full moons of the past two months, it failed to manifest, trying to judge whether the proper feeling was relief or even greater fear.

His own case was entirely different from Tularosa's

plight. One incident, so long ago, and while it marked him permanently, from his scalp to his inmost perception of the world around him, it was nothing Thorn had reason to believe would be repeated. Tularosans, on the other hand, were caught up in a cycle of attack, mystification, and foreboding that was self-perpetuating, wearing on body and soul.

It was a wonder, Thorn decided, that the townsfolk had not pulled up stakes and fled.

Which raised another thought. *Had* anyone departed from the village after the attack on Myron Decker, back in March? It could explain the recent lapse in homicides but would say nothing about June, July, September and October of last year, which also passed without killings. Thorn surmised that lawmen would have checked on shifty movements during months with no attacks, but he could take nothing for granted when it came to human negligence. Sometimes the simplest things eluded those who were entrusted with the most responsibility.

Thorn was mopping up his nearly bare plate with the final remnant of his toast when a disheveled cowboy-type entered the Lucky Strike. Before the waitress had a chance to reach him, he was shouting through the room to no one in particular, "They's been more killin' on the range! Word jest come in! A pair o' Messicans this time, out herdin' sheep!"

And he was gone, racing along the sidewalk to the next place he could find in need of grim news hand-delivered. Thorn finished his toast and coffee, donned his hat, and left some money on the table by his plate.

More killings meant a posse, and he meant to be a part of it.

His long strides took him toward the livery.

. . .

Heck Halliday felt numb. He'd prayed—not thought about it as he went to bed, but honestly for God's sake *prayed*— last night would pass without another incident, make it their longest stretch so far since all the bloodiness began, and now he knew that it had been in vain. Two shepherds slaughtered outside town, and that made eighteen total, putting everyone in town and on surrounding farms right back on edge.

They looked to him for help, before the county sheriff in Alamogordo, and so far he had failed them seven times. This made the eighth, and all that he could do was go through the same motions as before, head up a search and hope that something surfaced this time that would put them on the killer's trail.

Get on with it, he thought, quitting his office for the outer sidewalk where a crowd of fifty-odd townies had gathered, growing by the minute. They were muttering amongst themselves, somebody in the back ranks calling out to him, "Well, Marshal? What now?" as if it were all his fault.

Halliday raised his hands for silence, waiting while they settled down a bit. "You've heard the news," he told them, "or some version of it. What I hear, two Mexicans were killed last night, watching their sheep out on the flats a couple miles southwest of town. A rider from the Bar J found them. I don't have their names yet, so don't bother asking."

"That's nineteen," somebody cried. "Or is it twenty?"

"It's *eight*een," Halliday answered back, correcting him. "Don't make it worse than what it is."

"It can't *get* any worse," a woman's shrill voice challenged.

Halliday knew all of them but didn't bother putting names with voices. They were scared and had a perfect right to be, not knowing where the killer would strike next, inside of town or out, or which of them would be the next to die.

"I'm heading up a posse," Halliday informed them. "Riding out to see what happened, pick up any evidence or clues around the scene. I can take half a dozen men with steady hands, but not a mob that wants to mill around and trample everything. This ain't a sideshow, it's an organized investigation of a murder."

"Organized, my rosy red—"

"Shut up, Earl Withers!" Halliday shouted the heckler down. "I won't have that in public, and you won't be riding with the posse. Now, I'm taking Myron Colfax for the *Trumpet,* with his Stockwell camera to make a record of the scene and make sure we're not missing anything. We'll also be accompanied by Mr. Groom, our undertaker, to retrieve the bodies. That leaves four spots on the posse, to be chosen at my sole discretion and—"

"I'll ride along," a cool voice said. Halliday glanced off to his right and saw the stranger, Thorn, already mounted on a gray stallion, as if prepared to leave immediately.

"I'm asking for townspeople now," said Halliday.

Thorn said, "Or I can follow you alone. Whatever you prefer, Marshal."

"I won't have interference at the crime scene."

"And I wouldn't dream of it. No crime in riding through the country, though, the last I heard."

Halliday's cheeks were heating up, but he restrained himself from making any further empty threats. "Come if you want," he said, reluctantly, and saw most of the others ranged before him watching Thorn astride his horse, all dressed in black, with tied-down Colts. "Three more, then. Men with horses and a firearm, just in case."

A dozen hands shot up and Halliday chose three he knew as solid customers, not prone to going off half-cocked. They would obey him, if it came to that, and all of them were decent shots.

Not that he thought they'd find the culprit lingering over his kills this time. Whoever or *what*ever was behind the murders—he had given up on dogs at last, but still had trouble blaming any human for the hideous annihilation he had witnessed—he or it went prowling after dark and disappeared before the sun rose on another scene of carnage.

Goddamned spooky, what it was, and nothing Halliday had been prepared for when he donned his badge.

"All right then, that's the posse," he informed his audience. "Those coming, get your gear together and be ready within fifteen minutes. All the rest of you, go on about your business now and quit blocking the street."

Myron Colfax was a stout man in his latter thirties, his gregarious demeanor testimony to his role as editor and publisher of the *Tularosa Trumpet*. Riding solo in a buggy drawn by a bay mare, he had his Stockwell camera in back, together with a tripod and a suitcase full of dry plates ready for exposure at the murder scene. The other wagon coming with them, driven by a sallow young man with the village undertaker as his passenger, had two rough coffins in its bed, selected with the corpses sight unseen.

Before they got around to leaving Tularosa in a body,

Colfax fastened onto Gideon and asked if he could interview the new arrival as they made their way across the
plain. Thorn was determined not to give up much about
himself, but thought the newsman might be useful to him,
fleshing out the other local victims as they rode to meet the
latest pair.

Colfax began interrogating Thorn after they cleared the
village outskirts, pinning down his name and listing Boston
as his home address. Beyond that, Thorn managed to hold
the line while letting Colfax think that he was gaining
ground.

"I understand you've spoken to the marshal previously," said the editor.

"I'd call it roundabout."

"Meaning?"

"He came to me while I was eating at the Lucky Strike."

"And why was that?"

Thorn rolled his shoulders in a shrug. "I guess he heard
I was in town."

"And that would interest him because...?"

"Of what he heard about the reason," Thorn replied.

"Ah, now we're getting to it. And the reason is...?"

"I read about the murders here and thought I'd take a
look."

"Your reason being...?"

Colfax had begun to irritate him, but he thought a bit of
free publicity around the village couldn't hurt, and might
send someone else his way, if they were fed up with the
sluggish pace of the official manhunt.

"That's something I do," he told Colfax. "When word
comes in of something strange, what the authorities call
inexplicable, I sometimes feel a need to satisfy myself about
the cause."

After a moment's silence, Colfax asked, "Is this a hobby of some kind, or...?"

"Not a hobby in the sense of filling empty time," Thorn said. "It's my belief that anything can be explained, with proper understanding of the evidence. Whether that explanation fits within the staid parameters of present understanding is another question altogether. That does not concern me. I seek proof and follow where it leads."

"Indeed? And has your quest in Tularosa pointed you in a particular direction?"

"Not yet," Thorn replied. "I only reached your village yesterday, and when I asked about the marshal's files he voiced predictable reluctance. As it is, deprived of access to your own newspaper, all I know about the crimes is what has been reported from a distance, out of Santa Fe and Taos."

"Both of whom derived details from me—or, I should say, from the *Trumpet.*"

"That was my surmise."

"Well, Mr. Thorn, you're in first-hand on this one, though we hate to see another murder happening."

"Of course."

"As to the others, if you care to stop around my office later, I can fill you in on details of the crimes. Perhaps, in recompense, you'd tell me more about some of your other travels in pursuit of the unknown?"

"Be glad to," Thorn replied.

Ahead of them the marshal called out, "Getting close now." Mounted riders and the horse-drawn wagons all picked up their pace as they drew nearer to the murder scene, first notable by sheep grazing around on sage and desert grass as if nothing had ever happened there. It took another moment for the first of the two bodies to appear—

or what was left of it—and Thorn felt the day darken, even though the sky above was clear and crystal-blue.

"What would you say?" Halliday posed his question to Josiah Groom, the undertaker, who was crouched beside the savaged corpse with his assistant hanging back a yard or two.

"As in the past," Groom said, "it bears the outward indication of an animal attack. See how the throat and face were mauled, the body cavity opened and its internal organs randomly extracted, how the left arm has been *ripped* out of its socket, rather than truncated with a blade."

"About those organs, Mr. Groom," said Halliday. "Can you advise me as to whether any of them might be *missing,* as opposed to simply scattered?"

Groom considered that, straightened to scan the field around the dead Mexican's body, and replied, "I see most of the vitals present and accounted for. From that, I would exclude a portion of one lung, apparently devoured, and the heart—which being small, may have been flung a greater distance than we've presently surveyed. However..."

"Hearts were missing from the other scenes," said Halliday.

"Correct," Groom said. "Approximately half the victims, I believe."

"Well, shit."

Gideon Thorn was making mental notes as they moved on to view the younger Mexican. His handful of collected articles did not refer to hearts or any other missing organs by their names.

"I know these two," one of the riders—introduced on leaving town as Willard Poole—told no one in particular.

"The first one's Esteban Cardenas. This here is his son, Miguel."

"I don't recall them," Halliday replied. "They live somewhere around here?"

"Wherever their sheep were feeding, Heck. If someone owned the land, they'd pay a pittance for the short-term grazing rights or bargain for a share of what they made on wool and mutton before movin' on."

"So, transients," said the marshal.

"I suppose so. Been out here a month or so, driftin' around from one patch to another."

Something came to Thorn and he spoke up. "Whose land is this?"

All eyes turned toward the stranger on his gray. At length, Poole answered, "Jubal Stant. He's got about a thousand acres overall. What he don't graze himself, he'll rent to drovers passing through or sheepmen and the like."

"No animosity between them, then?"

"None Jubal ever spoke of," Poole replied.

"What are you getting at?" asked Halliday.

"You only have two options, Marshal. One, the killer wandered by on accident and chose these two to satisfy his appetite. Or two, he knew exactly where to find them and came out to kill this pair specifically."

"Hold on, now..."

"No insult intended to the landowner," said Thorn. "As Mr. Poole reveals, your Mr. Stant was not the only one aware of *Señor* Cardenas and son." Before the marshal could respond, Thorn shifted to the undertaker, asking, "Mr. Groom, can you advise us on the implements of carnage used?"

Groom glanced at Halliday; the marshal nodded back for him to go ahead. "Well, teeth, of course," said Groom.

"The bites are obvious and gaping, though I cannot say with any certainty what *kind* of teeth they were."

"Meaning?" Thorn pressed.

"As to distinguishing human from wolf, say, or some other common predator. As to the clawing, those were *talons*, up to four, five inches long by my guess, swung with extraordinary strength and cruelty, also employed to plumb the abdomens."

"And liberate the organs from within," said Thorn.

"Correct. The younger victim's injuries are all commensurate with those his father suffered, but his heart remains intact."

"In other cases, Mr. Groom, when there were two or more victims involved, was more than one heart missing?"

Frowning, Groom replied, "No, sir."

So only one's required per kill, Gideon thought.

He had already scanned the ground for footprints, finding that its dryness and the many trampling prints of sheep hooves made the search a futile exercise. A giant with a peg leg could have passed that way and had his tracks obscured. While Myron Colfax set about positioning his camera, preparing for the first of many shots to come, Gideon Thorn decided that he'd seen enough of this grim killing ground. Unless the undertaker could determine something more about the bites from further exploration at his parlor, or the heart missing from Esteban Cardenas should appear, they were tapped out.

The marshal sidled over, peering up at Thorn against the sun and lowering his voice. "I hope you don't know more than what you're telling me," he said.

"Nothing at all, Marshal. I merely posed a question from the evidence at hand: two dead, one heart removed."

Grudgingly, the lawman said, "I never noticed that before. Should've been obvious, I guess."

"Easy to overlook. You've had a ton of shocking information on your plate."

"Uh-huh. I still hold it against myself." He toed the dirt, then said, "About those files. I don't mind if you have a look, see if there's something else I missed."

"I doubt it, Marshal, but I thank you. I'll come by tomorrow, shall we say, when things calm down a bit?"

"Tomorrow." Halliday was nodding as he moved toward Colfax with his tripod, loading up a tray of flash powder.

Before it popped, Thorn had a head start back to Tularosa with his mind awhirl.

SIX

TULAROSA: HALF-PAST NOON

By the time Thorn got to town, returning Shadow to the livery and brushing down the horse himself, his stomach had begun to growl. His viewing of the crime scene had not put Thorn off his feed, in equal parts because he had not known the victims personally and because he was acquainted with the sight of bodies suffering indignities. It did not take a supernatural component for a person dying in the West to meet a slow, hard end—from outlaws, savages, a lynch mob, even Nature's predators and scavengers.

He wasn't blaming animals this time, however. What he'd seen was man's work. As to who the guilty party was, however—or if there were several involved—Thorn couldn't say.

He walked through town, postponing lunch until he'd ticked off all the other options on his list. The marshal's files were open to him, but he couldn't barge into the lawman's office and retrieve them, even if he found the door unlocked, while Halliday was busy at the murder scene. Same thing with Colfax, snapping photographs of the two victims *in situ* and unavailable for further questioning.

Which brought him back to lunch, and to the Lucky Strike.

As Thorn approached the combination of saloon and restaurant, he heard a scuffling sound within, accompanied by grunting, cursing voices. Drawing closer to the batwing doors, normally covered after closing by a stouter door of oak, Thorn peeked around the jamb and then retreated two long strides at sight of two men rushing toward him and a third resisting them, swearing and shoving back.

A moment later, all three cleared the threshold, two of burly build, sporting the garters of a barkeep or bouncer on their sleeves. The one they manhandled was younger, maybe half the age of his opponents, call it early twenties. He was largest of the three but could not handle both of them together in his present state, reeking of alcohol and slurring his abusive speech.

"Goddamn sonsabitches, shovin' me around," he railed, fists punching empty air. "Jus' put the liquor on my old man's tab, why don'tcha?"

As he spoke, a fourth man stepped onto the sidewalk, making five with Thorn included as a bystander. His slicked-back hair and bright red vest of silk suggested that he was an owner of the property.

"Your dad ain't picking up your tab," the new arrival said. "He's cut you off, as you were told *twice*, just this morning. You can come back when you've settled up your bill *and* you can pass the time without annoying any of my other customers."

"Customers?" the young man answered back. "You call

that rabble *customers?* Me 'n my dad *built* Tularosa, with a few more like us. *Built it,* damn you!"

"I can credit that about your father," Red Vest answered, "but I doubt you raised a finger doin' anything but boozing since you got the taste for it."

The drunkard's face turned red, nearly as crimson as the vest of his ejector from the Lucky Strike. He was about to answer when a fit of gagging overtook him and he heaved onto the wooden sidewalk, drawing groans and eye-rolls from his escorts out of the saloon. Thorn kept a grimace off his face but moved another long step backward from the young inebriant.

"Jesus," the owner said, "you are a stinkin' mess."

The drunk staggered, almost falling off the sidewalk, then dropped to one knee and retched again, this time staining his rumpled clothes. He put an arm out, braced himself against an upright pillar of the Lucky Strike's abbreviated balcony, and thereby kept from falling in the street.

"No more remarks to pass?" the owner challenged, with his muscle flanking him. "I didn't think so. Just remember what I told you. Don't come back until you've got the cash to settle up your tab and pay for each drink as you go."

The trio turned and left him, passing back inside. The drunk stayed where he was, gathering strength, eventually peering up at Thorn through dangling strands of hair worn long. "The hell you lookin' at?" he growled.

Thorn thought about responding, knew it was a waste of time, and stepped around the drunkard's steaming puddle to go in and order lunch, his appetite still undeterred.

The waitress from last night smiled at him hesitantly, shooting little glances toward the swinging doors, maybe remembering the tip he'd left beside his plate. Better to leave them smiling than annoyed, particularly when a waitress served the only public dining room in town.

She walked him to the same table where Thorn had eaten breakfast, with a good view of the street. Before he sat, she reconsidered, saying, "Mister, if you'd rather not be forced to look at—"

"No," Thorn told her. "Thanks. It's fine."

"Okay, then."

She presented him with what appeared to be the Lucky Strike's third menu, shortened from the other two with offerings for lunch. Thorn ordered chicken gumbo—"Cajun spicy!"—with a side of cornbread and his first beer of the day to get it started and an eye for berry cobbler as desert.

Distractedly, Thorn recognized the risk of falling into a routine in Tularosa, but the fact remained that he could either take meals at the Luck Strike or scout around for groceries and eat them raw, up in his hotel room. The latter thought held no appeal, and Thorn supposed that anybody seeking him would have no problem in the village, with its single restaurant and lone hotel available to travelers.

In fact, he thought—not for the first time—that it might work out to his advantage, if a local had something to spill. Meanwhile, the marshal's cautious thaw would offer Thorn at least a modicum of further information and he would proceed from there.

The waitress set a bowl in front of him that could have fed two starving men. Beside it sat a slab of buttered cornbread easily five inches to a side. His beer was cold, and while he stirred the gumbo with his spoon, letting it cool a tad, Thorn noted okra, rice, green peppers and onions with the chicken, plus fat chunks of sausage with a spicy Cajun smell.

He started with a bit of cornbread and a sip of beer, dipping the bread while gazing out the window. At the curb, if such it could be called, the young man recently ejected had regained his feet and slouched against a hitching rail, head drooping, hands stuffed into trouser pockets. Other than his age and size, approaching six foot five, strapping across the chest and shoulders, he could easily have been the standard drunk in any town Gideon Thorn had seen while passing thought the West. It was a shame to see him start so young, but he was not unique in that regard and it was none of Gideon's affair.

Taking it slow and savoring his gumbo, Thorn perused the dining room. Of nineteen other tables, only three were filled, all couples dining quietly and concentrating on their food. Along the bar, two drinkers occupied the only stools in use, seated widely apart to keep the bartender in motion, drifting back and forth between them. Overall, the air was somber, not what Thorn remembered from the night before, or even during that day's breakfast.

Murder often put a damper on the appetite.

Thanks to the Powers That Be for his immunity.

While Thorn had visited communities that lived under a threat of violence, he'd never put down roots in one. Boston had crime of course, and plenty of it, which included homicide. But those were random acts, or else the work of gangs known to police. Some went unsolved—too many, if the truth be told—but that was urban life. Some bad men got away with crimes indefinitely; others were arrested swiftly and dispatched to prison or the gallows. Would-be victims with the wherewithal to help themselves moved into neighborhoods strongly patrolled, and in the case of certain millionaires, employed private security. The rest were left to take their chances in the streets and in their homes.

He was a world away from Boston now, and no mistake.

Outside, two horses sidled up to the young drunk, their riders somber looking in the shade of wide-brimmed hats. One of the men addressed the tippler, leaning on his saddle horn, and got an answer back. From his expression, as he glanced across at his companion, Thorn assumed it was sarcastic.

More trouble, he surmised, determined to stay out of it.

Thorn couldn't tell whether the new arrivals knew the drunk or simply wanted to remove him from the hitching rail's vicinity, to tie their horses up in peace. A moment later, when they both dismounted and approached him more aggressively, he got the sense that it was something personal.

He flagged the waitress and she veered off course to answer him, approaching with a question. "Everything okay, I hope?"

"Couldn't be better," Thorn replied. "I'm wondering about that fellow who was put out earlier."

As if there might be several, she leaned to have a look and said, "Oh, him. That's Declan Stant."

"Any relation to the rancher, Jubal Stant?"

"His one and only son," she said. "Likes drinking, mostly when he can't pay up."

"And those men speaking to him?"

"Couple of his daddy's hands. One on the left is Arnie Something. I don't know the other's name."

"Thanks very much."

"And while I'm here..."

"Another beer would definitely hit the spot," Thorn said.

He ate and watched while Arnie Something and his pal tried talking Declan Stant down from his latest binge. It was an old story, prodigal son, and hirelings of his father were constrained in how far they could go handling Junior. By the time Declan was nodding, pointing down the street toward something, possibly wherever he had left his horse, Thorn's interest in the encounter had begun to wane.

Still, Jubal Stant intrigued him for his link, however tenuous, to last night's victims. And if they had drifted, other farmers might have dealt with them as well. Somewhere along the line, a quarrel might have led to killing, but Thorn knew well enough that wasn't how a racial incident normally played out in the West.

If there were whites involved, they had an edge over the region's other residents. Longstanding tenants of the land, the Indians and Mexicans, had been displaced at gunpoint or compelled to live in a subordinate condition. Ex-slaves, spreading outward from the postwar South, were greeted with a wide field of emotions ranging from contempt or outright hatred to small pockets offering cautious acceptance. The Chinese—"celestials" or worse, to whites—were low-end labor from the far side of the world, feared for their strangeness or despised for their acceptance of rock-bottom wages, welcomed for the most part only when they dealt in opium or Eastern whores.

The net result: whenever violence erupted, whites on one side and the other red, black, brown or yellow, it was normally assumed that whites—often mislabeled as the "native born"—were in the right, acting in self-defense. Murdering Esteban Cardenas and his son over some range dispute would not require a gross charade of teeth and claws by moonlight, when it could have been enacted at high noon, in downtown Tularosa, with impunity.

The waitress brought his beer, the trio moved beyond his view outside, and Thorn turned back to finishing his meal.

Ten minutes later, while Thorn used the last piece of his cornbread as a swab to trap the gumbo's stragglers, he saw Myron Colfax pass by in his buggy, bearing dry plates to develop at the *Tularosa Trumpet*'s office. Thorn cleaned up and paid up, downed the last dregs of his beer, and went outside to see if Marshal Halliday had made it back from visiting the dead. By then, there was no trace of Declan Gantt or his two escorts to be seen along the thoroughfare.

As he expected, Halliday had ridden back with Colfax and was in his office, door open to let the pent-up heat escape, seated behind his desk and jotting notes onto a foolscap writing pad. Thorn rapped his knuckles on the jamb and asked, "Bad time, Marshal?"

Halliday laid his pencil to the side and said, "As good as any on a day like this."

"Eighteen," Thorn said.

"And nothing that would put us on the killer's trail. We have to wait another goddamn month, and all for what? To hope we catch him in the act?"

"I can't help thinking something from the crimes must tie them all together, or at least a few of them."

"Well, if it does, I don't know what in hell it is. I've got the files here for you. Maybe you can see something I've overlooked."

Halliday pushed a stack of slim manila envelopes across the desk toward Thorn. Gideon picked them up without examining them in the marshal's presence, nodded thanks, and was prepared to leave when Halliday called after him

"You asked a couple good questions today, about the hearts and landowners."

"Speaking of that," Thorn said. "I take it you know Declan Stant?"

"He's Jubal's son, not good for much but pulling corks. I've locked him up for public drunkenness and fighting three, four times. His daddy always bails him out."

"A good-sized boy."

"You've met him?" Halliday frowned now.

"I saw him getting thrown out of the Lucky Strike today, when I got back. A couple of his father's riders came to pick him up."

"That's one arrest he dodged, me being out of town."

"Mostly embarrassing himself, from what I saw. Thanks for the files. Okay if I return them in the morning?"

"Fine. If I was going to spot something fresh, I would've seen it before now."

Thorn walked back to the Tularosa House, checked with the clerk for any mail addressed to him and found it nonexistent, then climbed to his upstairs room. The maid had come and gone, but none of Thorn's belongings were disturbed, a piece of thread he'd draped across the closet's handle still in place where he had left it.

Sitting in the single chair, he spread the marshal's files out on his bed by date, with February of last year the farthest to his left, proceeding on along the mattress to the death of Myron Decker, three months earlier. There was no envelope for the two shepherds yet, and Thorn had seen as much as anyone was going to observe at their death scene. If something popped out from their past, he hoped that Halliday would share it with him, or that

Myron Colfax would exchange it for some bit of trivia on Thorn.

Each file in turn repeated what he had already gleaned from newspaper accounts, but there were tidbits that had missed the press, contributed by Halliday, by friends or neighbors of the dead, and tips from locals with suspicious minds.

The Carmodys were separated by nine years in age and seemed to have no enemies—or no one who admitted to disliking them, at least. From Halliday's handwritten notes, Thorn saw that Frank had been the first to die, his heart ripped out while he was in the barn, along with other limbs and organs scattered. Halliday assumed that Judith had gone out to find her husband when he missed her call to supper and was ambushed in the yard, gutted, her head torn off and dropped into a water trough they used for stock. How that had led to killing feral dogs was anybody's guess, but Thorn supposed it was the best that Halliday could do to calm an outraged populace.

The lovers, Spence and Paulson, had been found together, naked, near a local fishing hole. Their clothes were laid aside, if not exactly folded, indicating that they'd stripped and were enjoying one another when disaster struck out of the night. That time, the killer fled with Marlon Spence's heart, torn from his chest and never found.

Joe Margulies had died alone, slopping the hogs. Newspapers noted that his left leg had been carried off, but they forgot to mention—or were never told—about his missing heart.

Next up, on May's blue moon, the Ostman family. Father Cole had lost his heart in that raid, while the lone survivor, privy-hider Justine, never glimpsed the fiend who orphaned her. She *did* remember certain sounds, however:

shrieking from her house, accompanied by growling like the snarls of a large, powerful animal.

The brothers Jamison went down in August of last year, with Cabel's heart and Brent's left kidney missing from the scene. Thorn wondered if the predator was eating them, preserving his mementos somehow, or employing them as sacrificial offerings. He'd run across a sacrificial cult, working across the Tex-Mex line, but nothing in their operation had suggested imitation of a prowling beast.

As far as Brent and Cabel, Marshal Halliday had logged their conflicts with a neighbor's eldest son. He'd pulled the suspect in for questioning, determined that the argument revolved around a girl who teased Brent and his rival equally, and finally released the other boy for lack of evidence. In any case, nothing had linked the young Lothario to any of the other homicides.

And so it went with the attack on Nasker's Hardware— Steve's heart taken from the scene, along with what Halliday branded "lady parts" from wife Helene. Deputy Decker, first to die in 1875, had been another heart donor, surprised and butchered while he rattled doorknobs on March twenty-third. A village drunk had threatened him, because Decker had jailed him once, but he was back in lockup on the night the officer was torn apart, his head, one arm, and kidneys vanished with his missing heart.

Enough for stew, thought Gideon, and grimaced at the thought.

His knowledge had increased, but he would have to read the files again, more slowly, to absorb their full detail. Meanwhile, he craved fresh air and thought it was a perfect time to visit Myron Colfax at the *Tularosa Trumpet.*

SEVEN

A tiny bell rang overhead as Thorn pushed through the doorway of the *Trumpet*'s office, with the printing plant in back. Colfax was somewhere in the rear but came out when he heard the bell, wearing an apron and a green eyeshade that gave him the appearance of a faro dealer.

"Mr. Thorn! You've caught me in the act, developing my dry plates from the scene of the unfortunate...um...incident."

"Sorry to bother you," Thorn said. "I can come back another time."

"Not necessary, sir. You mentioned looking at back issues of the *Trumpet*?"

"That's exactly what I had in mind."

"Your luck is holding." Colfax pointed to the west wall of his shop, behind a narrow counter set between the lobby and his desk, where ranks of newspapers were shelved in cardboard binding, dated on the spines. "The dates you seek are there. Please use the working table to your heart's content, while I continue with the photographs. Say thirty, forty minutes at the most? And then, perhaps we'll have another opportunity to talk."

"Sounds good," Thorn said, pushed through the little waist-high swinging gate, and went to scan the volumes of back issues while Colfax ducked out of sight.

The *Trumpet* was a modest weekly paper, four pages per issue, mirroring the fact that Tularosa was a quiet place except in times of turmoil. Each slim volume spanned three months, so Thorn took down the four spanning last year and set them on the table, perching on its wooden straight-backed chair.

The Carmody attack had come on February 1, a Sunday, and commanded headlines when the *Trumpet* kept its normal Wednesday publication schedule. From the article, Thorn drew a sense of horror radiating from the page but no hard information on the crime. The next week's issue covered Marshal Halliday's campaign against stray dogs, producing no link to the double homicide but salving public fear to some extent. By Wednesday the eighteenth, the killings were bumped down below the fold, and on the twenty-fifth Colfax simply reported "Still No News."

The Spence-Paulson attack had fallen on a Tuesday night and thereby missed inclusion in the *Trumpet*'s issue on March fourth. Colfax made up for that on the eleventh, nearly all of his front page devoted to the crimes, including trivia about the lovers' grades in school, their throttled aspirations from the future, and another pogrom launched against the village's surviving feral dogs. Over the next two weeks, while apprehension lingered, rumors of rogue Apaches fleeing the San Carlos Reservation intervened and gave the locals something else to fear.

Opening volume two, Thorn skimmed through April, finding only that authorities reported no developments. It seemed to be accepted that some animal or pack of beasts had been responsible for the attacks and had moved on. That supposition shattered on May first, a Friday, and demanded nearly two full pages of reportage in the *Trumpet* on May sixth. Joe Margulies had died alone, the first assault to only claim a single victim, but the tally stood at five and panic ramped to fever pitch. A final hunt for dogs, expanded to include wolves and coyotes, turned up nothing. Speculation shifted to a homicidal maniac at large, and once the full moon link was noted, the assassin instantly became a "lunatic."

Apparently, no one had figured out that May had *two* full moons that year. It was a rare phenomenon and unaccounted for in Tularosa. When the killer struck again on Sunday the thirty-first it sent shock waves through Otero County and beyond. The Ostman massacre had doubled any prior body count and also left the killer's sole survivor, for all the good that did. Thorn made a mental note to ask about their farm, together with the Carmodys', and see if he could get a closer look.

Two months of silence, with declining coverage in print, and then the Jamisons were taken one day after Colfax ran his last issue of August on the twenty-sixth. Eleven dead meant further panic, guns sold out at Nasker's Hardware in the village—and a touch of irony when that became the slayer's next target after a fresh two-month hiatus. Butchered on a Monday, Steve and Helene Nasker, with their children, filled the *Trumpet*'s issue on November twenty-fifth. It was a grim Thanksgiving for the residents of Tularosa, most of them thankful for simply living through the holiday.

Returning to the shelf, Thorn fetched down volumes one and two for 1875. The luckless deputy had died on

Tuesday night, March twenty-third, too late to make the next day's headlines, but his death was covered fully on the thirty-first, with smaller stories dribbling out over the next four weeks. Next up would be Eladio Cardenas and his son, awaiting coverage next Wednesday unless Colfax opted for a "special" printing for their case.

"Find what you need?" the editor asked Thorn, returning to the office from his backroom hideaway.

"Some of it," Gideon replied. "But what I really need is more insight into the victims. Who they were, how they behaved, their friends and enemies, any connections linking them."

Colfax slipped off his eyeshade, sat behind his desk, and said, "A *quid pro quo*, agreed?"

"Agreed."

"In that case, let's begin."

Colfax had stepped into the story of a lifetime and he knew it. While he mourned sincerely for the victims, both as individuals and members of his own community, he would have been a fool to overlook his personal advantage, planted on the front lines of a case that would make history. A well-read journalist, he'd never heard of anything even remotely similar in the United States, and nothing on the Continent since Gilles de Rais, back in the fifteenth century, of Countess Báthory two hundred years behind him. This was *new*, and when the case was finally concluded—if it ever was—Colfax would be the first to write a book-length story of the frontier crimes.

Gideon Thorn intrigued him, too: a driven man with secrets in his past, perhaps the subject of another series or a separate volume?

"The Carmodys were normal farming folk," he said. "No children living, but they'd lost a couple over time, still-births, and gave up trying as I understand it. They were likable enough but didn't socialize that much. Their Saturday routine prevented them from lying on the farm indefinitely, undiscovered."

"So, no enemies?" asked Thorn.

"If so, they kept it to themselves. The marshal asked their neighbors, who reported finding them. Nothing came up."

"And what about the lovers?"

"Marlon and poor Mary Lou. A truly tragic case."

"But raising possibilities."

"With reference to jealousy, of course. The marshal and our county sheriff, Adam Rooney, both looked into that angle. Myron appeared to have no open rivals for the girl's affection, though it's always possible they overlooked some clandestine admirer."

"And the parents?"

Colfax hesitated. "That's a shocking thought."

"Is it? Back east we read of parents killing children frequently, for varied reasons."

"In the slums, of course, from drunkenness, but—"

"Also incest or inheritance—it cuts both ways—and scriptural reaction to defiance, among other things."

Colfax could feel his head shaking before he fully registered Thorn's statement. "No," he said, with perfect confidence. "Not here in Tularosa."

"It's impossible?"

"For all intents and purposes I think so, yes." But why did Colfax feel his certainty evaporating in the face of Thorn's cool stare?

"Joe Margulies?" the visitor inquired. "Enemies? Any vices you're aware of?"

"He was just fifteen years old!"

"Some boys are fathers by that age. John Clem was twelve when he enlisted with the Union side and killed a Rebel colonel at Chickamauga."

"But still—"

"All right, pass over him. Tell me about the Ostmans."

Colfax felt the interview had slipped away from him, becoming an interrogation with himself cast as the subject. "They were sturdy farming folk," he said, almost defensively. "Well liked by all who knew them in the neighborhood."

"And came from where? How long ago?"

For that, the newsman had to pause and think. "About five years ago," he said at last. "From somewhere in Ohio, I believe."

"No enemies back there? Outstanding debts they failed to pay before departure?"

"Not that I'm aware of, Mr. Thorn."

"And no involvement with the Mormons there? They've had to deal with bloody persecution in Ohio, going back some forty years."

"There are no Mormons in Otero County."

"Was the farm successful? Any evidence of strife within the family itself?"

"As to the first point, they were doing fairly well. As well as anyone the past few years, considering the local droughts, flash floods, what have you. Marshal Halliday might tell you more about their personal affairs, but I'm aware of no complaints."

"And as I've seen, the *Trumpet* publishes reports of all local arrests, lawsuits, and so forth."

"Absolutely."

"But if there was an investigation that did not proceed to court..."

"Nothing of that sort, I assure you."

"One big, happy family."

"From all appearances, within the limits of the life they chose."

"Would you know if they owned the land outright or rented from another?"

"They acquired it through the Homestead Act, like most farmers throughout the Territory."

"No encumbrance, then? No debts worth mentioning?"

"Not to my knowledge. If you asked the bank in Alamogordo..."

"The Jamisons," Thorn interrupted him. "Just normal youths again, I take it?"

"Yes."

"What do you know, if anything, about their skill with firearms?"

Colfax shrugged and answered, "They were farm boys. Knew enough to hunt and keep the pot full, I suppose."

"Both carried rifles and had time to use them before dying. What does that suggest to you?" Thorn asked.

"It puzzled me in August and still does today. Brent had his father's .30-30; Cabel brought a little .22."

"Still does the job," said Thorn, "if shots are placed correctly."

"I suppose the pair of them were frightened, taken by surprise, and missed."

"Was either of them sweet on any local lovelies?"

"Nothing in that line was mentioned during the investigation. Surely—"

Thorn dismissed it with a wave and asked him, "What

about the Naskers? They were active merchants and first victims in the village proper. Any troubles you're aware of there that didn't make it into print?"

"I am not in the business of suppressing news, sir!"

"But you might not speak ill of the dead, with Tularosa's reputation riding on the line," Thorn said.

"I strive to tell the *truth*!"

"Of course. Nothing on record about any customers delinquent in their payments to the store, for items bought on time? No animosity with possible competitors?"

"Nothing that came to light." Aside from his resentment of the stranger's tone, Colfax was moved to wonder if his own investigation of the murders was sufficient. Had he overlooked the obvious in some cases, rejecting likely motives out of hand without pursuing them to any firm conclusion?

"Finally," Thorn said, "at least before last night, we have the deputy."

Colfax was nodding. "Myron Decker," he confirmed.

"A part-time carpenter, I understand?"

"Correct."

"And how long had he been a lawman?"

"Only since the Nasker killings. Marshal Halliday wanted another man to help him cover Tularosa day and night. Myron had time to spare and volunteered."

"Three months then, more of less, between those murders and his own."

"Within a day or two," Colfax agreed. Should he be taking notes? At least pretending that he was the interviewer, Thorn the interviewee?

"In his time as deputy," Thorn asked, "how was he?"

"I'm not sure I follow."

"Was he conscientious? Did the badge go to his head at all and make him throw his weight around?"

"Nothing like that. I'm sure he knew it was a temporary job and that his livelihood depended on the good will of the town."

"According to the *Trumpet,* Decker only made the one arrest."

"John Norville. He's a drunk. There's no point sugar-coating it."

"He wasn't happy, being locked up."

"Never has been, likely never will be, but he sleeps it off."

"And was in custody the night that Decker died."

"Was slaughtered. Yes. No question he was under lock and key."

"No friends who might have acted from revenge, on his behalf?"

"Norville's a hermit," Colfax said. "He lives away off, up in the Sierra Blancas. Rarely surfaces except on Fridays, for his weekly bender. Sleeps it off and picks up his supplies on Saturdays."

"His source of income?" Thorn inquired.

"That's the funny part. He has a silver claim. There's not much to it, but it keeps him going, hoping that he'll hit the mother lode one day."

"Just one last question for the moment: have the murder farms been occupied by new tenants as yet?"

Colfax was thrown off-balance, but he knew the answer. "No, sir. Neither of them yet.

The Ostman girl is staying at a neighbor's place for now. The search for relatives continues."

"Very good," Thorn said, already on his feet and turning toward the exit.

"Wait! Our interview—"

"Has been concluded for the moment," Thorn replied. The tiny bell sounded as he opened the door. "I may have other questions, but for now it's *adios.*"

Thorn was a regular by now, for dining at the Lucky Strike, and it was pushing dinnertime when he left Colfax, village merchants shutting down a little earlier than usual since two more bodies had been added to the growing list. Foot traffic on the thoroughfare was thinning out, and those who lived outside of town were wrapping up their business, heading out on horseback or in wagons bearing goods they'd bought.

Tonight, Thorn guessed, the village would be relatively quiet, and the tavern's drinkers would be casting glances at each other, wondering if someone close at hand could be a killer. He'd seen other towns endure the same thing, with a range of variations, and it seldom ended well: strangers were eyed suspiciously, neighbor mistrusted neighbor, even close-knit families might suffer unexpected rifts.

And through it all, a killer moved at will.

The same waitress from Saturday met Thorn and led him to a small table for two, this time set in a corner of the dining room, well back from the street scene where dusk was rapidly descending. "We're closing early," she informed him, as she handed Thorn a menu.

"Sunday hours?"

"Nope. The killings. Business isn't what the manager would like."

"Quite understandable." He scanned the cardboard sheet and said, "I'll have the porterhouse and baked potato, with the collard greens and biscuits. Coffee on the side, and skip desert."

"Yessir. Shouldn't be long."

Thorn counted only three tables in use besides his own, with half a dozen solemn drinkers at the bar. No one was visible in the casino, separated from the dining room in theory by an open doorway strung with beads. The Lucky Strike's soiled doves would be upstairs, either with customers or spending time alone inside their cribs. Small wonder that the man or men in charge would choose to close and start fresh on the morrow, when the tang of murder had begun to fade.

A question that he had not asked as yet occurred to Thorn: with the two shepherds dead, what happened to their sheep? Would relatives be coming to retrieve them? And if so, from where? Had they been Mexicans, in fact, or registered citizens of the Territory? Did their lease include provision for the landlord to receive the herd if they were killed?

Thorn seriously doubted whether that had any bearing on the crime, but overlooking it until that moment meant that he was tired, slipping, and needed rest. Sleep felt inviting, even after what he'd seen that morning, but he wasn't ready to discard the day just yet. After he dined, Thorn planned to read through Marshal Halliday's collected files once more, make sure that he'd missed nothing, before he returned them in the morning.

And what had he learned so far? Eighteen people, all "normal" within local standards, had been butchered, with a heart taken away from every murder scene. That aspect jogged grim memories from his research: hunters gnawing on the hearts of deer or other wildlife kills, some Indians and other primitives around the world devouring the hearts of honored human captives to ingest their courage. It was not unknown by any means, and once had been considered common among certain tribes, but in the present day and place it signaled some sort of insanity.

Assuming that the killer was in fact a human being.

That conundrum resurrected Thorn's disjointed, fragmentary memories of early childhood. He had no idea precisely what his parents or his brother suffered on the night they died, although he pictured sudden death, his mother's case excepted. Nothing he had ever dredged up from his mind suggested a *devouring,* and yet the crime was blamed upon an animal.

Thorn was distracted by his meal's arrival, pleased to find his appetite intact despite his morbid turn of thought. In fact, he had lived so long with the images of loss, the mystery surrounding them, that they no longer frightened him as an adult. Instead, he longed for answers, explanations, still convinced they waited for him somewhere in the West.

And Tularosa? Might whatever happened there place him a little closer to the truth?

Chewing a bite of steak, medium rare, Thorn knew that he would have to wait and see.

EIGHT

JUNE 20, 1875

After breakfast at the Lucky Strike—bacon and pancakes, with a mug of coffee—Thorn bought a beef sandwich for the road and walked down to the livery. He paid for two more nights and saddled Shadow, put the sandwich in his saddlebag with other gear, and made sure his canteen was full before he left the village, heading north. A half-mile out of town he veered a little to the west and let the stallion set his own pace for the nine-mile ride ahead of them.

There was no hurry visiting the murder ranches. Neither one of them was going anywhere.

The ex-Carmody spread was farther out, and so was Thorn's first destination. He was not expecting much, if anything, but had refreshed his memory from Marshal Halliday's sparse files last night, as well as his brief conversation with the *Trumpet*'s publisher. The Carmodys, those "sturdy farming folk," had bought their land from predecessors—failed farmers named Dugan, late of Ireland—and hoped to make a go of it where the previous owners had not. It seemed their luck and strength of will might turn the place around until disaster struck and claimed their lives.

Crossing the open landscape toward his goal, Thorn thought about the two Carmody children that were stillborn. That was tragic in its way, but not unique on the frontier by any means, where medicine was often primitive or nonexistent and the nearest hospital might be a week's ride distant, if the parents could afford it. In the territories, Thorn reflected, birth came down to luck and circumstance.

Three hours after setting out from town, he found the spread that he was looking for. The house was of a fair size, probably constructed for a larger family before the Carmodys moved in, with three bedrooms, a parlor, kitchen, dining room, and privy in the yard. The door was shut but wasn't locked, granting him entry to the house without a key.

Based on the layout and dust patterns on the floor, some of the furniture had been removed after the murders, likely claimed by neighbors when no kin arrived to take possession of the property. That meant nothing to Thorn, convinced as he already was that robbery played no part in the crime. Whoever or *what*ever targeted the Carmodys as victims served some burning drive aside from human greed.

It felt strange, moving through the musty, dead space of a house once occupied, its tenants now deceased. There were no ghosts in residence, as far as Thorn could tell, but sixteen months was long enough for any spirit to move on, if they existed in the first place. Thorn guessed that his Aunt Drusilla might have tried a séance to extract whatever energy remained, see what some latent shade might have to say about the crimes, and while he had participated in a ritual or two at her behest, communing with the Other Side that way had never truly suited him.

Some things, he felt, were best left undisturbed.

And ghosts, from what he'd heard, were sometimes known to lie.

The house held nothing for him. Neither Carmody had died within its walls, and once his passing inventory was completed, Thorn went back outside. Shadow grazed along the fence of a deserted corral, cropping grass from a vestige of shade. Thorn angled toward the barn, its door wide open to the weather as it had been left after the bodies were removed.

Inside, revealed by daylight spilling through the doorway, Thorn saw ancient rusty bloodstains on the barn's dirt floor. Without knowing the story of what happened there, he could have said that whoever was injured in the barn had not survived. Nobody spilled that much blood from his veins and lived to tell the tale. As for the rest of it, Frank Carmody's remains had been removed by whoever was sent from town to gather them, most likely undertaker Groom. The nature of the crime was not discernible today, so long after the fact, but death had touched this place and left its mark behind.

Thorn had already passed the spot where Judith Carmody was slain, between the house and barn. Over the intervening months, weather had scoured the yard and cleaned away all traces of her fate, but Thorn knew she had died in the same manner as her husband, set upon and mutilated as if by a beast. Only the killer's bite marks and the depth of its claw wounds suggested size, and even that was vague approximation. Wolf-sized, at the very least, which had precipitated random killing of the region's feral dogs. The fact that none of them were known as killers, much less man-eaters, had not allayed the fear driving their slaughter.

But the purge had failed.

Thorn thought back to the case of his own family once more, had no idea if there'd been anything resembling an investigation at the time. From what he gathered, long years afterward, it was assumed that a rogue grizzly bear had stormed the cabin in a killing frenzy. No one could explain where it had come from, why it was not hibernating with the others of its kind, or how it chose the home of Aaron Thorn to sate its thirst for blood.

Despite a total lack of evidence, Thorn lingered in the yard, around the spot where he presumed that Mrs. Carmody had fallen and been mauled. He stared away into the distance, scanning the horizon, wishing something would occur to him, some psychic flash to solve the case, but nothing came. A faint breeze, warm and dry, ruffled the fringes of his hair beneath his high-domed hat, and then moved on.

"I guess we're finished here," he told Shadow. "One other stop, and then we pack it in."

That morning, before going to the Lucky Strike, Thorn had returned the borrowed files to Marshal Halliday with thanks. He'd mentioned visiting the murder farms and caught the marshal's frown, but Halliday had offered no objection in the end. "Be careful" was the sum total of his advice, as he got back to writing up his summary of the Cardenas homicides.

Hoping that Thorn would turn up something he had missed? Or counting on the fact that nothing new or startling would be found?

Halliday's office was elective, Thorn had learned, a two-year post, with an election coming in November. If he solved the killings, any rival trying to unseat him would be seen as tearing down a local hero. If he failed...well, maybe it was time for someone else to have a go.

Thorn was indifferent to politics beyond the broad issue of who became the U.S. president next year and what that meant for Dixie in the throes of Reconstruction, the stain of corruption in Washington, and the ongoing depression sparked by the Panic of 1873. More specifically, a local race in Tularosa held no interest for him whatsoever, other than its impact on solution of the recent brutal crimes. Heck Halliday appeared to be a competent lawman, for all his failures in the present case. Would his successor, if Halliday lost the race, be an improvement or a detriment?

With any luck, if Thorn could crack the homicides, it made no difference.

He had imposed a limit on himself, had no plan to become a county resident and linger overlong, gnawing the mystery as some dogs cherish an old bone. Waiting around for next month's full moon on July eighteenth held no appeal for him, particularly since the killer had skipped over that month, last summer. Once Thorn had set that pattern he could wait forever, one month to the next, still lingering if no fresh leads emerged. It was, as far as he could tell, this week or never for the Tularosa terror.

The Ostman ranch was three miles south of Carmody's and closer in toward town. Along the way, he ate his sandwich from the Lucky Strike while Shadow paced the miles away, Thorn's mind anticipating what he'd find at the next stop. Four dead and one survivor, now removed. The one who'd lived, Justine, was four years older than he'd been the night his family was massacred, but she'd seen nothing from the backyard privy if her story was the truth. It might not be, but Thorn was put off by the thought of finding her and squeezing her to see if she had managed to suppress some painful memory.

The girl was six years old. Wherever she might be, he planned on leaving her alone.

The countryside due west of Tularosa shifted as he traveled, desert giving way to grassland, trees sprouting in clusters. More of it would serve as grazing land after a decent rain, a prospect more likely in Otero County than some other parts of the Southwest. Thorn's almanac told him that the district averaged sixty-odd rainy days per year, with twenty-three inches of snowfall the mean during winter. It was still hot and dry during summer, but its normal peak of eight-five degrees for mid-July was far better than Arizona Territory's or Nevada's, both nearing 120 degrees Fahrenheit.

That kind of weather drove snakes underground and pushed men to their limits, pursuing their dreams—or their nightmares—on ranches, on mountains, in mines. The end result was often mayhem, sparked by greed or lust or pure frustration, but at least the bloodletting was comprehensible.

In Tularosa, though...

Thorn understood the Donner Party, feeding on their dead when they were forced to winter in the Rockies, twenty-eight years earlier. He grasped the motive of another Colorado cannibal, prospector Alfred Packer, who'd turned to eating other members of his expedition during last year's winter, then escaped from custody before he could be sentenced and remained at large. Survival was a motive few had power to resist, but that was not reflected in the Tularosa crimes.

What Thorn had seen was savagery, a kind of bestiality that made him question whether he was looking for an animal, a human, or some grim amalgamation of the two.

Worldwide, he knew, most cultures on the planet had their tales of shapeshifters—humans imbued with special powers or the victims of a curse who transformed into animals, either at will or when a call of nature overwhelmed humanity. Ancient Egyptians, Greeks and Romans worshipped hybrid gods bearing the heads of animals. Medieval Europeans lived in dread of werewolves dominated by the moon. Far Eastern legends spoke of men and women turning into foxes. When conquistadors and colonists invaded the Americas, the aborigines already had their tales of skinwalkers, shamans who transformed into wolves, coyotes, bears, or other forest denizens to prey on men.

But were the stories true? How could the human form reshape itself into a hairy quadruped and roam the wild, even with aid from magic that conventional religion presently denied? Was it a fantasy, as distant from reality as stories that maintained the sun was Helios, son of Hyperion, who drove his fiery chariot across the daylight sky?

After the slaughter of his family, the mystery surrounding it, and all that he had learned since then, Gideon Thorn could not decide. Part of his quest was a pursuit of that specific answer—something, anything, to satisfy his mind.

Until he found it, he would never be at peace.

The Ostman spread had more of everything: a larger house and barn, more outbuildings, and two corrals instead of one. At first glance, that reflected affluence, but nothing

Thorn had heard so far suggested any monetary angle to the murders. It would take more research than his time allowed to trace the Ostmans back to their Ohio roots, discover why they'd left the Buckeye State to settle in New Mexico, although it seemed that Mormonism played no part in it. And once religious persecution was removed, what else remained?

The Ostman raid had been the first time more than two victims were slain, the first killings performed indoors, the first that missed one member of the target family. As yet, Thorn didn't know what any of that meant—if anything at all—but he was working on it, seeking any stone still undisturbed that he could flip and find an answer hiding underneath.

Nothing was inexplicable. *No* mystery was destined to remain unsolved.

Shadow approached the homestead cautiously, pensive, Thorn trying to communicate a sense of calm and put the stallion more at ease. When he dismounted in the dooryard, Thorn made no attempt to tie the horse, but rather let it roam at will, graze where it would, and call to him if it felt anything amiss.

Communication went both ways.

Before he breached the slaughterhouse, Thorn walked around behind it to the privy that had saved Justine Ostman. It was a stout two-holer, offering accommodation to the children, with a bunch of *Tularosa Trumpet*s tacked up to the wall for use as tissue. Thorn did not venture inside —the smell was fading after seven months' disuse, though still repugnant—but he stood in the doorway and faced the house, closing his eyes, imagining a midnight hurry call disrupted by the sound of screams and growling from within the home.

It chilled him and his eyes came open of their own accord.

Time to explore the house. He walked back to the front porch, tried the door, and found it unlocked like the Carmodys'. This time he saw no evidence of any furniture being removed, but that was just a guess. If anything was missing, Thorn could not imagine what it might have been or where it would have fit. He saw a life uprooted in Ohio and transported to New Mexico, repotted in a new house, then disrupted by a midnight massacre. Whether grim death had trailed the Ostmans from their former state or waited for them here, it had come close to wiping out the family.

The four who died were sleeping when it started, probably oblivious to Justine slipping out to use the privy. In the master bedroom blood spattered the walls, the floor, even the ceiling, where the slayer ran amok, mauling husband and wife in a demented frenzy, heedless of the sounds he made or of his victims' fruitless cries for help. The murdered brothers, Zebulon and Jonas, tried to flee in darkness but were overtaken, downed and ripped asunder before they could exit from the house. Their blood trail marked the hallway leading from the bedrooms to the kitchen, where the chase had ended in another bout of carnage.

Did their injuries suggest cannibalism?

Taking that as fact, it meant both killer and his prey belonged to the same species.

Not a given, Thorn decided, though pure logic also posed the question: *What else is there?*

Animals, of course, although the situation called for one able to turn a doorknob—and defeat the lock if it had been engaged, a likelihood after five other murders in the area.

Only a fool would leave his house unlocked under those circumstances, and no evidence suggested that Cole Ostman was a fool. And since there was no indication anyone had forced the lock, that meant the killer either had a key or was adept at picking tumblers.

More questions to be asked in Tularosa. Had the Ostmans shared a key with any of their neighbors, for emergencies? Had they concealed a key somewhere outside the house, and if so, who had known where they should look for it? Did anyone in town or on outlying farms have training as a locksmith?

What about Steve Nasker at the hardware store? Would he have peddled locks and keys? Would he perhaps have been adept at opening the locks he sold to customers? There was no reason to assume an overlap between the Ostman and the Nasker massacres, but any lead Thorn could hypothesize, at this point, was worth investigating further.

Exiting the bloodstained house, which he surmised would be a hard sell to prospective tenants now at any price, until its rooms were sanded and repainted, Thorn glanced off across the landscape northward, toward a ridge perhaps a mile distant. A solitary rider sat atop the rise, immobile, the bare suggestion of a face turned toward the Ostman farm.

Pretending that he hadn't seen the man, Thorn crossed the yard to Shadow, reached inside one of his saddlebags, and found the spyglass that he carried there. The telescope's casing was brass and it had three collapsing sections that extended eighteen inches overall. With its refracting lens the glass could bring a distant object into sharp relief, perhaps enough for Gideon to single out the horseman whom, he now felt reasonably sure, was watching him.

But when he raised the telescope and focused over Shadow's saddle, trying not to be too obvious about it, Thorn had missed his chance. The rider had already turned away from him and was descending on the far side of the ridge, only his hat, back, and his buckskin stallion's rump still visible.

Gideon knew it was a waste of time to mount and take off in pursuit. Even if he could overtake the stranger, what was he to say? A neighbor, even someone casually passing by from Tularosa, would be curious about a visitor examining the Ostman farm. It was entirely natural for he—or *she,* Thorn couldn't rule it out—to pause and watch the interloper poking here and there around the murder-blighted property.

One good thing: Thorn was fairly recognizable in black, perhaps enough so for a curious inhabitant or someone with a useful lead to contact him in town. With that in mind, he put the telescope away and mounted Shadow, steering him toward Tularosa and another visit to the Lucky Strike.

NINE

In ordinary circumstances, Thorn disliked being predictable. But in his present situation, limited to dining at a single restaurant *and* hoping someone from the town might contact him with further information on the local string of crimes, he was prepared to make an exception.

After dropping Shadow at the livery, seeing him brushed down, fed and watered, Thorn stopped at the Tularosa House to drop his Winchester and saddle bags, then crossed the street to sample supper at the Lucky Strike. The menu hadn't changed, but rather than repeat himself, Thorn ordered the beef stew with something labeled "Texas toast." In practice, that turned out to be more of the same thick toast he'd had with breakfast on Saturday morning, richly buttered, while the stew came in a large bowl like the one that held his gumbo that same day, at lunch. Aside from hearty chunks of beef, it had potatoes, carrots, onions, celery and peas mixed into thick, rich gravy that could almost hold his spoon upright.

Thorn had consumed one steaming mouthful when he spotted Myron Colfax entering the dining room. The editor scanned faces, more than half the tables filled this early evening, then passed the waitress with a nod and made a beeline straight for Gideon.

Damn it!

Instead of grimacing, Thorn spooned another mouthful of his stew and spoke around it. "Mr. Colfax."

"Mr. Gideon. May I intrude?"

"Too late to ask."

The newsman blinked at that, then chuckled to himself and sat across from Thorn. The waitress circled back and Colfax ordered coffee, black. "About that promised interview..."

"Promised?"

"Um, well, perhaps the promise was implied."

"Or possibly *inferred*," said Gideon.

"In any case, is this an inconvenient time?"

"You see me eating dinner."

"Ah. Well, if it's possible to schedule an occasion, possibly tomorrow morning..."

"Don't know where I'll be," Thorn answered honestly. "You'd best get on with it."

"Perfect!" Colfax produced a pocket notebook and a stub of pencil, licked the pencil's tip, and frowned as he considered his first question. Finally he asked, "Is it correct to say you travel in pursuit of mysteries to solve around the West?"

"Not quite." Thorn dipped his toast and took a bite, chased it with coffee from his steaming mug. "The cases I investigate, like Tularosa's homicides, have been reported in the press. I go where the events have already occurred, not simply wandering around and hoping I'll discover something."

"But you focus on ... how shall I say it? The unusual?"

"Would you rate any unsolved mystery as *usual?*"

"Um...I suppose not, if you put it that way."

"Well, then."

"Have there been many others like our own unfortunate events?" Colfax inquired.

"An accident may be unfortunate," Thorn said. "Murders are *crimes*. In answer to your question, other cases I've investigated have involved fatalities, but nothing on this scale."

Colfax put on a solemn face. "The toll on such a small community is taxing. How do you propose to solve the case where others, paid professionals, have failed?"

Thorn saw the trap and sidestepped. "First," he answered, "I do not propose to solve the case—or, rather, cases, since you now have eight attacks with eighteen murdered victims. Second," he continued, stretching it, "I make no criticism of your village marshal or the county sheriff, whom I haven't even met. They are elected officers and have applied themselves to the solution of these crimes as thoroughly as possible, from what I've seen. All over the United States, including major cities coast to coast, police are faced with unsolved crimes."

Colfax cocked one eyebrow, giving his face a vaguely Luciferian expression. "Well, in that case, Mr. Thorn, what is your contribution to the case?"

"Fresh eyes," Gideon said, before he filled his mouth with stew once more. "And my unique experience."

Colfax jotted that down while Gideon worked on his meal and sipped his coffee. When the editor was satisfied he'd caught the quote verbatim, he asked Thorn, "And what exactly is that personal experience?"

This was the part where Gideon felt bound to hedge,

without entirely burying his past. A hint of what he had survived might bring some contact from the woodwork, ready to impart a crucial piece of information formerly withheld from the impassive law.

"When I was two years old," he told Colfax, "my family was slaughtered up in Kansas Territory. By an animal, investigators claimed, although they never found out what it was or where it came from, much less where it went when it was finished. Since then, all the way through school and growing up, I've been committed to discovering what happened that night and investigating other cases where it seemed authorities were baffled."

"When you mention school..."

"Most recently it's Harvard, Class of '73."

Colfax blinked twice at that, jotted his note, and forged ahead. "As far as solving other cases go, can you cite some examples?"

"Once again, misquoting," Thorn replied, and dipped another piece of cornbread in his stew, about half finished now and still holding its heat. "I've said that I *investigate* them. In some cases I have satisfied myself regarding answers, but that doesn't mean there was a trial and someone went to jail. Some of the cases I've become involved in were not crimes. In one, the only suspect killed himself without confessing. Others...well, they still require more thought."

"And what about your family?"

"The verdict stands as it was handed down in 1854."

"But *your* inquiry—"

"Is ongoing. After twenty years and counting, you'll appreciate that any witnesses and evidence are difficult to find."

"If not impossible," Colfax replied. "Forgive me, Mr. Thorn, but would you possibly consider that pursuit a personal obsession in the mold of Captain Ahab?"

Melville's whaling novel, *Moby Dick*, had gone to press the year before Thorn's birth. He'd read it at age nine and thoroughly enjoyed it as a fictional adventure, but he saw no parallel between the peg-legged captain and himself.

He told the newsman, "Your comparison is inexact. First, Ahab is a character of fiction and he knew precisely which whale claimed his leg. I lost three members of my family, my parents and my older brother, killed before my eyes."

"By what, sir?" Colfax challenged him.

"Alas," Thorn said, raising another spoonful of his stew, "a two-year-old's perception of a vicious and chaotic action rarely is precise. My vision from that time—firelight and swirling snow, dark fur, long fangs and claws, my parents' sacrifice that I might live—leaves me without a clear impression of the beast."

His mind adding, *If beast it was.*

"If I may ask you one more thing..."

"I'm sorry, Mr. Colfax, but my dinner's getting cold." Not strictly true, but close enough. "And I have work to do when I'm done here. Tomorrow is another day."

"More hunting, Mr. Thorn?"

Gideon smiled at him and said, "It never ends."

Heck Halliday was standing at his office window, in the dark, when Thorn passed by, between the Lucky Strike and his hotel. He watched the man in black stride past him on the far side of the street, not glancing over, passing locals who were scurrying to get indoors before full dark descended over Tularosa.

Logically, they should have known that they were safe tonight and for the next month, till another full moon rose over Otero County on July eighteenth. So far, the killer had hewn strictly to his lunar schedule, sometimes skipping months, but killing only on those nights when a full moon lit up the nighttime sky.

That said, why would a normal Tularosan trust that schedule with his life, the safety of his family? If anything was clear about the crimes, it had to be the slayer's homicidal mania. A man—or men, Halliday couldn't rule it out —who had descended that far into madness might desert their chosen ritual at any time, deciding they should only kill on Sundays, say, or on the second Tuesday of each month.

Halliday was no alienist, or what new-fangled publications had begun to label a *psychiatrist*. He'd worn a badge for fifteen years, in one town or another, and could understand the workings of a normal human mind. People were driven to excess by greed and lust, by sudden fury and revenge, by alcohol and opiates. In nine crimes out of ten he'd tracked the cause to money, sex, or anger—and sometimes a mixture of all three. The deaths in Tularosa, though, were something new and ghastly in his personal experience.

And Thorn? What was his interest in the protracted suffering of strangers?

Halliday had marked him as a suspect when he first rode into town, but that idea had quickly dissipated. Thorn had not been present during any of the murders but the last attack, and Halliday had easily confirmed his presence at the Tularosa House when that occurred. The stranger's private explanation to him, seeking links or evidence related to his family's annihilation in the 1850s, had a ring of truth about it but the incident could just as easily have sparked unhealthy feelings in Thorn's mind.

Something to watch for, as if Halliday wasn't already swamped enough.

On top of all the killing and the criticism he'd received for failing to curtail it, now he had to think about November and the race to keep his job. Elections lowered public service to a popularity contest, frequently won by whoever could tell the most convincing lies. A lawman running on his record needed something he could brag about, and standing by while some demented bastard slaughtered eighteen citizens was definitely in the minus column when it came to bagging votes.

His opposition in the coming contest, Asa Faulkner, had no law enforcement background beyond serving as a bailiff for the county court in Alamogordo. He'd never jailed a lawbreaker, except for those who had been cited for contempt of court. These days, Faulkner, age fifty-six, was puttering around his house in Tularosa, planting vegetables in his garden, likely thinking that he'd been too hasty in retiring. What else was he suited for except to wear a badge?

And now he had the perfect issue: eighteen unsolved murders, maybe going on forever if the voters granted Halliday another two-year term to laze around his office, poking at the evidence and solving nothing. Faulkner likely couldn't manage any more, but he could *promise* anything. That was the way to win elections when the rubes were riled and frightened.

Halliday had hoped Thorn might discover something in

his files to crack the case, but no such luck. Unless the man in black was lying to his face, Thorn seemed to honestly believe that Heck had done his best. Which wasn't saying much, all things considered. Losers could be thorough. Winners took a leap of faith and made it count, but Halliday had no idea what that might be.

What would he do if he were voted out of office in November? Halliday had been a lawman for so long, and prior to that a bouncer in saloons, that it was all he knew or felt that he was capable of doing. He would have to move, of course, find somewhere else to sell himself, and that would be a chore, considering the reason for his leaving Tularosa.

Who wanted an officer whose last great case had gone unsolved with eighteen dead?

Another way to go, of course, was *solve* the goddamned thing before Election Day. That meant a new beginning, going back to start all over with the Carmodys, and maybe Thorn could help him if asked. What harm was there in that? Maybe tomorrow, bright and early, but without disturbing Gideon at breakfast, getting off to a bad start.

His only other hope was waiting for July and seeing who died next.

No messages awaited Thorn at the hotel, and why should there have been? He'd sent a wire to Boston from El Paso, tipping off Obi Magoro to his latest travel plans, but Tularosa had no telegraph office and any letter sent from Massachusetts, if the African were so inclined, would have to make its slow way overland, most likely missing Thorn after he'd left the village. Only if he stayed around into July was there a likelihood of mail, and Gideon had no such plans.

Back in his hotel room, chair propped under the door-knob, Thorn decided he would shave tonight and save time in the morning. He used a boar-bristle brush, soaking it before he stirred a quantity of Colgate Demulcent Shaving Soap and lathering his face. While that soaked in, he stropped his straight razor and then began the ritual of scraping cheeks, jawline, and throat. Experience had taught Thorn that his concentration on the process and his visage in the mirror gave him time to organize his thoughts.

And that was something that he badly needed now, before he spent another hour on the Tularosa crimes.

His tour of the murder farms had reinforced impressions of the killer's brute ferocity, without imparting any further information toward a capture. Thorn had feared as much, but still felt that the trip had been worthwhile. Tomorrow, if he had a chance, he would attempt to get a closer look at Nasker's Hardware Store downtown. That was the third crime carried out indoors, but more importantly, the first in Tularosa proper, as the killer lost his fear of working in the settlement itself.

And what would Gideon discover, if he were allowed to tour the shop?

Nothing, perhaps, but if he didn't make the effort...

His mind returned unbidden to the rider he'd caught watching him, while he was at the Ostman spread. Logic still told him there was nothing to it—and the killer had no way of knowing Thorn would go to see the ranch that day, unless Colfax had leaked his plan to someone else in town. Thorn's brief glimpse of the rider through his telescope assured him that it was not Colfax spying from the ridge top, but who *had* it been?

There was a theory, held among some law enforcement officers, which claimed that certain criminals revisited the scenes of former crimes, deriving satisfaction from reliving where they'd been and what they'd done there, playing out the graphic scenes within their minds. Others, the experts said, sometimes attended funerals of the very victims they had murdered. In a village Tularosa's size, Thorn knew, most of the residents would turn out for a burial, but going back to crime scenes from a year or more ago was something else.

Thorn wished now that he'd seen the distant rider's face, to recognize him if they met again or passed each other on the street. Too late, he thought again of giving chase but realized it would have been a futile exercise.

What were the odds that his observer was entirely innocent, a simple passerby? Considering the area, how rarely farmers seemed to leave their plots of land except to fetch supplies from Tularosa or to visit one another, Thorn made it even money that the watcher had been checking on the Ostman farm deliberately, either looking out for Thorn or trying to discover whether anyone at all had renewed interest in the crimes.

In which case, not pursuing him had been a serious mistake.

Thorn made a last swipe of the razor underneath his chin, was just about to rinse and wipe its blade clean when the window to his right imploded, shattering in fragments with a crash. He heard the rifle shot a heartbeat later, as he dropped for safety to the floor amidst the window's broken glass. A second shot followed almost immediately—time enough for someone on a rooftop opposite to pump a rifle's lever-action or to aim the second shot out of a double-barreled weapon.

While that shot punched through his door and out into the hallway, Thorn was rolling, picking up small nicks from shattered glass, and made it to the small room's single lamp, just out of line from where the sniper must have been. He doused it, moved in darkness toward the window, and peered out into the night. A human form flitted across the Lucky Strike's low parapet across the street, then dropped from sight.

Thorn snatched his gunbelt from the bed, took time to lock his door after he cleared it, and was buckling on his pistols by the time he reached the hotel's stairs. He had not taken off his boots before he started shaving, more a lucky accident than anything, but he was conscious of forgetting to retrieve his shirt before he reached the lobby, clad from the waist upward only in long underwear.

The clerk was gaping at him as he passed, starting to ask Thorn, "What was—" but he did not tarry to explain. A Colt was in his right hand as he cleared the exit onto Tularosa's thoroughfare, and he immediately sprinted for the Lucky Strike, intent on circling around behind the tavern, looking for some access to the roof, then barging in if he found none outside and trying to discover who had fired the shots.

Instinct told Thorn that he was already too late, that anyone who knew the town from long experience would have escaped his aerie and would be long gone by now, but Gideon still had to try. Whether the watcher at the Ostman farm had been coincidence or not, the hotel shooting—whether an attempt to kill him, botched by haste, or simply someone's notion of a warning—meant that he was onto something, even if he had no idea what it was.

Thorn saw no one on the street as he was crossing, hardly a surprise one night after the latest double murder, but he heard piano music coming from the Lucky Strike. Business as usual at the cantina, even if its customers were winnowed to a minimum. Thorn wondered if the tinkling music would have drowned out gunfire from the roof, decided he would likely have to ask inside, and then he heard a loud familiar voice call out to him.

"Thorn! Hold up there! What's going on?"

TEN

Heck Halliday was giving up and writing off this Sunday evening as far as any further study on the murders was concerned. He couldn't put them out of mind, but sitting in his office after all the shops had closed and stragglers from the village's two churches had gone home to bed made no sense whatsoever.

Not that he could manage to forget the killings just by walking back to his small house a half-block over from the town's main street; far from it. Halliday was confident they would keep preying on his mind and that he'd dream of them tonight, the victims trooping past him with their mutilations, those who still had heads or faces blubbering at him through blood to solve the case and save himself at the same time.

Halliday lived alone, no wife to keep his supper warm or tell him it would be all right tomorrow, when he viewed the problem in a new day's light. He'd married briefly, twenty years before, but typhus cut that short and left him bitterly convinced that he was meant to lead a solitary life. The vagaries of working as a lawman reinforced that supposition, since no woman cared for being constantly uprooted and transported to another town, when work ran out in one after the next. He was a drifter, in effect, seemingly doomed to live in no location any longer than it took to put a lid on crime or upset some rich bastard who demanded special treatment.

There were none of those in Tularosa, but the murders had defeated Halliday. He could admit that to himself, even if he maintained a bold face for the populace at large. He knew no more about the crimes today—or very little more, at least—than when they'd started, sixteen months before. How many more townspeople had to die before he got a clue and traced it to a suspect?

Maybe dozens, said a bitter voice inside his head. *Maybe you'll* never *crack it.*

Cursing at himself and at his circumstance, Halliday straightened up the papers spread across his desk, leaving them stacked by case with no mix-ups, and pushed up from his rolling wooden chair. The cells in back were empty, as they had been for the past eight days approaching the full moon. Even the town's worst drunks were loath to be locked up and left alone during the countdown to another round of bloody homicides. The whole town knew that Halliday went home by ten o'clock, whether he had a prisoner in custody of not, and now that death might strike inside the very village, even in the jail, why take that chance?

Halliday left the office, locked the door behind him, and remained in darkness on the sidewalk for a moment. There were only four streetlights in Tularosa, two at each end of the village thoroughfare. They were torches more than anything, wide metal cones set atop nine-foot wooden poles and filled with pitch that was ignited within thirty minutes after sundown and left blazing through the night, until it burned away and darkness settled in once more. The village lamplighter received a pittance to prepare and light them of an evening but did not make a second round to keep the torches burning through the late night hours, on till dawn. Eying the flames, Halliday estimated that they had another hour or ninety minutes left before the last of them went out.

He tried in vain to make his mind a blank, was turning from his office doorway, when a shot rang out above him, somewhere to his right. Halliday tracked the sound instinctively, heard glass breaking across the street, and was in time to see the second muzzle flash blaze from a rooftop corner of the Lucky Strike, directed toward the Tularosa House. The *crack* came to his ears immediately afterward, sound traveling more slowly than the wink of gunfire.

Halliday drew his well-worn Colt before he realized that he was reaching for it, one more instinct he had picked up in his long years as a lawman. He had no idea who'd fired the shots, but guessed without much doubt who the intended target must have been: the only stranger presently in Tularosa, and the only person other than the marshal who was digging into eighteen unsolved homicides.

As Halliday began to cross the street, still watching the cantina's roof, a thought passed through his mind: *Why fire at Thorn and not at me?*

The answer came immediately after, grimly obvious. No one who lived in Tularosa or Otero County thought their marshal was about to solve the crimes. Thorn, on the other hand, remained an unknown quantity. Someone might have decided that he needed warning off, or maybe they were trying to eliminate him altogether.

Halliday was halfway to the Lucky Strike when movement on the sidewalk of the Tularosa House distracted him. He turned, saw Thorn emerging from the lobby, dressed for strolling from the waist down, with a pistol in his hand. Stopping, Halliday called out to him, "Thorn! Hold up there! What's going on?"

Thorn spun to face the marshal, then immediately lowered his six-gun. "You heard the shots," he said, stating the obvious.

"I *saw* the second one," said Halliday, and pointed with his Colt. "Up there."

"I glimpsed a shadow from my window, too," Thorn said.

"Are you all right?"

"Clean misses," Thorn replied. "Come on, we're wasting time."

"If you're joining me—"

"I'm looking for whoever tried to kill me, Marshal. Either come along or stay out of my way."

Halliday stepped in front of him, Colt angled halfway toward the ground between them. "Things are done the legal way in Tularosa," he insisted. "No damn vigilantes running through the streets."

"Relax," Thorn said. "I need to question whoever it was, unless we stand around and let him get away."

"All right, you're deputized," said Halliday. "Don't shoot him if you can avoid it."

"I feel better now," Thorn quipped.

Before they reached the tavern, Halliday asked him, "No chance to make out who it was?"

"A moving shadow, nothing more. I likely wouldn't know them anyway." He hesitated for a beat, then added,

"Somebody was watching me this afternoon, out at the Ostman ranch. I tried to glimpse him through a spyglass but he turned away. Male rider on a buckskin stallion, but I couldn't tell you any more than that."

Halliday frowned and said, "I know a couple animals like that, offhand. We can look into that tomorrow."

"But tonight—"

"We'll split up. You want inside or outside?"

"I'll take the roof," Thorn said.

"There's dual access, from the second floor and by a ladder on the back wall," Halliday replied.

"See you up there," Thorn said, and sprinted for an alley on the left or south side of the Lucky Strike, pitch darkness there, with ample room for one or more would-be assassins to conceal themselves.

Thorn drew his second pistol as he ran, prepared for anything as he approached the black maw of the alleyway. Before he entered, pressed against the nearby wall, he paused and listened for the sound of footsteps nearing or retreating, but he only heard the marshal's now, as Halliday approached the Lucky Strike's front door.

Wishing him luck, Thorn turned into the alley, crouching slightly as he moved to make himself a smaller target, noting light at the far end from a round moon one night past full. His mind skipped back to legends of the skinwalkers, wondering if they were supposed to change only on one night of a given month, then told himself that no half-man would use a rifle if he were possessed of fangs and claws.

Thorn reached the far end of the alley unopposed, waited another beat, then swung around to face the back-side of the Lucky Strike. He saw the ladder mounted on its wall, a few feet to the left of the backdoor—which suddenly swung open just as he approached it.

"Freeze!" Thorn shouted, and a young man burdened with a heavy tub of soapy water did as he was told, gaping into the twin barrels of Gideon's matched Colts.

"D-d-don't shoot me, Mister, p-p-please!"

"You work here?"

"Y-y-yes, sir!"

"See anybody coming out this way, the past ten minutes?

"N-n-no, but I been w-w-workin' in the k-k-kitchen."

"All right, go about your business."

Visibly relieved, the young man dumped the contents of his tub without proceeding any farther from the door, splashing his shoes and trousers with the used dishwater, then ducked back inside, leaving the door ajar.

Thorn eyed the ladder, put away his guns, and started his ascent. An enemy atop the roof could pick him off with ease, one shot to end it, but Thorn had no other choice.

Hand over hand, he scrambled toward the rooftop and whatever waited there.

The predator curses himself for being hasty, wasting what had seemed to be a perfect opportunity. He's never been much of a shot at long range but felt bound to try it anyway. The second shot, an impulse, had been foolish, but he'd hoped at least to drive the lesson home and put the goddamned snooping stranger off his trail.

Now, has he ruined everything?

The smart move, after last night, would have been to lie low for another month or even two, then go back on the prowl.

Logic informs him that the black-clad stranger he had glimpsed at Ostman's spread would not remain in Tularosa for another lunar cycle, waiting to find out if more murders would follow. He is bound to leave sooner or later, travel on in search of other cases, other unsolved mysteries across the West.

So simple, but the predator has messed it up.

Again.

The man who's hunting him will stay at least a little longer now, to find out who's responsible for shooting at him. All the predator can hope for from this bungled night is to escape unseen and make his way back home. He will be safe there, more or less, until the panic and attendant danger fade once more. During that time he can relax and savor his last outing, play the scenes over and over in his mind.

Soft flesh. Hot jets of blood. The dying screams of man and boy.

Father and son, he has discovered, and that makes it all the sweeter, as if he's wiped out another family. The heady sense of power almost overcomes him, but he staves it off in time to keep himself clear-headed, living in the moment as he flees the Lucky Strike's rooftop, scrambling down and off into the night.

His buckskin stallion waits behind the former hardware store, abandoned now. He hears it whicker in the darkness and responds, a soft and lulling voice to calm the animal at his approach. He must be cautious riding out of town, draw no attention to himself, or Marshal Halliday might mount a full pursuit by moonlight. That could be disastrous, even with a running start. The predator needs to be safe at home, not roaming aimlessly over the desert with a posse on his heels.

Don't worry, says the voice inside his head. *No one can hurt you.*

But if that's the case, why does he fret over discovery? Why not reveal himself and flaunt his power to the world?

Because he is not *perfect* yet. He still needs two more kills to guarantee the immortality he has been working toward, and then he'll be unstoppable. He can go anywhere. No territory can confine him. He will be a legend in his own time, carving bloody swaths across the land.

And it is only fair. He has survived so much to reach this point.

He is *Yenaldooshi*, the skinwalker.

Has not the shaman told him so?

The stallion shies a little, then catches his scent. The predator returns his rifle to its saddle boot and mounts the animal, clutching its reins. A slight nudge from his heels and it begins to trot along behind the shops lining the east side of the thoroughfare, not running yet in case someone awakened by the rifle shots peers from a window and discovers them. Nothing suspicious must arouse a chance bystander as they flee.

Passing the livery, the stallion smells strange horses and cannot help whinnying, but then they clear the northern outskirts of the village and the predator clucks to his beast and snaps the reins, leans forward in his saddle as the stallion picks up speed. It knows the way home, galloping beneath the moon that still pulls on its rider, but without sufficient strength to make him change.

Good luck for the buckskin. Good luck for both of them.

The predator regrets his mission as a failure, but at least he tried.

Whatever happens next is Fate, and there is no escaping that.

. . .

Six feet below the rooftop's parapet, Gideon Thorn stopped on the ladder, listening, then surged over the top. He landed in an awkward crouch but caught his balance, drew his right-hand Colt and swept the roof, still half expecting to be shot or rushed by whoever had tried to kill him in his hotel room short moments earlier.

The empty rooftop yawned at him.

He circled once around it, vaguely conscious that the faint piano music from downstairs had stopped, presumably when Marshal Halliday entered the tavern with his pistol drawn. That was enough to dampen any party, much less on the night after a double murder when the town was still in shock and mourning for the latest dead.

Thorn wondered if whoever was beneath him, on the second floor—the whores and their distracted customers—could hear him tramping overhead. What if the sniper had escaped that way, using the low trapdoor that Thorn now saw almost dead center in the flat plane of adobe, granting access to the floor below?

In that case he was gone, perhaps about to meet the marshal in the ground-floor barroom or to hide out in one of the Lucky Strike's cribs. They might be forced to search the whole establishment, another waste of time if they had missed the shooter coming in.

The roof gave Thorn a new perspective, looking over Tularosa, but the Lucky Strike was not a tall building, such as the ones he'd seen in Boston and New York. Even Harvard's campus buildings towered over the cantina, putting Tularosa in perspective. Peering down upon its unpaved central street and lower rooftops showed Thorn nothing but the torches at each end of town and certain windows showing lamplight that were dark before the shots.

Moonlight was useful to him as he made a second circuit of the roof and wound up at the corner where he'd seen a hulking shadow duck from sight, after the gunfire capped his shave. He saw two small, metallic objects glittering and knelt beside them, peering closer without touching them.

A pair of cartridge cases lay within a foot of one another, where they'd fallen when ejected from the shooter's rifle. That meant a lever-action weapon, since the older Colt revolving rifle held its spent rounds in a cylinder until the shooter dumped them loose.

Thorn was about to take a closer look when he was suddenly distracted by a scraping sound behind him. Turning with his pistol raised, the other leaping to his left hand, he saw Marshal Halliday emerging from the roof's trapdoor, staring down the twin Colt barrels.

"Point those somewhere else if you don't mind," Halliday said.

Thorn holstered his revolvers, rose, and pointed toward the cartridge cases at his feet, saying, "He fired from here."

"Same corner where I saw the second muzzle flash," the lawman said.

Halliday knelt beside the spent shells as Thorn had, stared at them for a moment, then pronounced, "Rimfires." He picked one up, peered closely at its base, and added, "It's a .44 Henry."

Thorn knew the rifle Halliday referred to. Pioneered in 1860, it held sixteen rounds specifically designed for it and had been issued to some Union Army troops during the Civil War. In all, some fourteen thousand were produced before the New Haven Arms Company stopped making them in 1866. Some were in service with the U.S. cavalry on frontier duty; many more had found their way into civilian hands.

"Do you know anyone who packs a Henry around Tularosa?" Thorn inquired.

"I've got one in my office," Halliday replied. "I'm certain of a couple others, but that doesn't mean I've seem 'em all."

"More questions then."

"I'll deal with that tomorrow morning," Halliday assured him. "No point waking anybody up tonight."

"Just out of curiosity, who are they?"

"One is Reverend Silas French."

"A rifle-packing minister?"

"He's Free Will Baptist. Found my deputy's left arm lying across his altar back in March. Besides, this *is* the territorial frontier."

"And what about the other Henry?"

"You already met him," Halliday replied. "Ace Donovan."

"The barber."

"Right."

"Good with a rifle and a blade."

"Well, he can shave," the marshal said. "I haven't seen him shoot. He keeps the Henry at his shop. For an emergency, he says."

"No claws, though," Thorn observed

"Not that I've noticed, when he cuts my hair." Halliday hesitated, then picked up the second cartridge case and put both in his shirt pocket. "I'm not sure what to do with these," he said. "Maybe if I had some way to compare a firing pin to markings on the cases..."

Thorn knew that Halliday was dreaming, given science in its present state. Marks from a bullet mold had convinced one British murder suspect to confess in 1835, but no slugs had yet been matched to a particular gun's barrel by the rifling marks. As for the tiny dents created by a weapon's firing pin, no method of comparing them was known to criminology.

Thorn kept the gloomy prospect to himself, thankful that Halliday was treating the attack with all due seriousness. Questioning the town's known Henry owners was a start, but nothing more.

Meanwhile, Thorn had to see about a change of hotel rooms.

ELEVEN

JUNE 21, 1875

Thorn got his share of odd looks at the Lucky Strike on Monday morning. Even though the night crew had gone home, word of the shooting incident had reached the tavern's other workers and, in fact, had made the rounds of Tularosa by sunrise. Thorn had the faint aroma of a marked man now, even the breakfast waitress sparing with her smile after she seated him.

In spite of last night's action—or because of it—Thorn felt as if he hadn't eaten in a week. He ordered two fried eggs with extra bacon, pancakes on the side with maple syrup, and a mug of fresh black coffee to ensure that he stayed wide awake. The waitress nodded while she took his order and seemed grateful to escape as she retreated toward the kitchen.

Switching rooms had been no problem, since the Tularosa House was short on guests. It never did great business at the best of times, and recently the village's adverse publicity had cut down on the normal flow of travelers who chose to stay the night. As far as Thorn could tell, his only neighbors in the fourteen-room hotel were two traveling salesmen and a young surveyor passing through. Thorn's new room, at the hotel's rear, was more or less identical to what he'd left, minus the bullet holes. He'd pulled the drapes first thing and wedged his chair against the door, as previously, before climbing into bed with both Colts and his Winchester to pass a quiet night.

The thoroughfare was coming back to life as Thorn received his breakfast, thanked the waitress, and dug in. He ate with purpose, tasting and appreciating everything, but focused on last night's events and what they meant as far as his pursuit of Tularosa's moonlight murderer.

Whether the shots were fired by Gideon's quarry or an associate—a twist that he was loath to contemplate, hoping the village only held one maniac—it meant he had unsettled someone and provoked them to dissuade him from continuing his hunt. Whether the shooter meant to miss or not, Thorn got the message.

But he wasn't backing off.

If anything, the sniping had increased his personal determination to press on.

Thorn mulled over the Henry rifle problem. Marshal Halliday had managed to identify three of the guns in Tularosa, one of them his own. Thorn didn't peg the local barber as his would-be killer, though he could not rule it out, and he was also skeptical about the Baptist minister he'd never met. Beyond the minister's profession—which, in Thorn's experience, was *not* a guarantee of any special rectitude—it seemed unlikely that the full-moon killer or a sidekick would have placed a murder victim's arm inside the preacher's church. That struck Thorn as an insult, a *defilement* of what Christians called the house of God, not something that a minister would do unless his mind was seriously out of order.

Then again, the killings spoke of madness, so the argument became a circular and self-defeating one. A crazy man might do most anything.

The waitress made another pass, refilled Thorn's coffee mug, and as she left he saw the marshal standing on the far side of the street, watching a wagon pass before he came across. *What now?* Thorn wondered, but he knew Halliday would be entering the Lucky Strike and more than likely heading for his table.

Set on finishing his meal, Thorn ate the final piece of bacon, chased it with the last bite of his second egg, and was already mopping up the last traces of syrup with a wedge of pancake when the door opened and Halliday came toward him, waving off the waitress as he passed her by.

The marshal sat without an invitation and remarked, "Looks like you're winding down here."

"Just about." Thorn sipped his coffee, waiting for the lawman to explain his presence.

"I'm on my way to see Ace Donovan," he said at last.

"You mentioned that last night. And then, the minister."

Halliday nodded. "When I got to thinking, though, I figured maybe you might like to come along. Being the one who almost took a slug and all."

Thorn risked the bare hint of a smile. "Would this be something like collaboration?"

"Just don't rub my nose in it," the marshal answered back. "Ready to go?"

. . .

Ace Donovan was finishing an early-morning haircut when they reached his shop. The customer was portly, florid-faced, and sported a luxuriant moustache as if to compensate for thinning hair on top. Halliday greeted him as "Mr. Gregson," did not bother introducing Thorn, and took one of the empty chairs beside the barber's door. Thorn sat beside him, waiting silently while Donovan finished a joke about a farmer's daughter and a salesman caught out in a storm.

When Gregson left, departing with a nod to Halliday, the barber asked, "Who's next?"

"We don't need any work this morning, Ace," the marshal said. "A few quick questions ought to see us gone."

"Well, fire away," said Donovan, relaxing in his barber's chair.

"Funny you'd say that," Halliday replied. "You hear about the shooting overnight, down at the Tularosa House?"

"Word gets around, Heck."

"Someone took a couple shots at Mr. Thorn, here, from atop the Lucky Strike."

"Do tell."

"They missed, as you can see."

"Lucky," said Donovan, and smiled.

"Thing is," said Halliday, "they used a Henry rifle."

The barber raised an eyebrow. Said, "You reckon it was *me*."

"No reason to believe it, Ace. I have to ask around with anyone who keeps one, though. You understand."

"There's Preacher French," said Donovan.

"Next on my list. Your shop is closer to my office than his church."

"Well, you already know I've got a Henry. Haven't fired

it in a couple years, at least. You want to see it? Maybe sniff the barrel?"

"Guess I ought to, for the record. Meaning no offense, Ace."

"Hell, none taken. Just doin' your job. I'll be right back."

Donovan rose and ducked into the backroom, where he kept the two bathtubs. Thorn reached down casually to release the hammer thong on his right-handed holster, noting from the corner of his eye that Halliday had done the same.

The barber returned in a minute or so, holding his Henry rifle at port arms and handing it to Halliday. The marshal took it, sniffed the breach without pulling the lever-action down, then took a quick whiff of the weapon's muzzle. "Oil," he said.

"I keep it clean and lubricated," said the barber.

Halliday poked at the muzzle with a fingertip, then rubbed the finger with his thumb. "Not fresh," he said.

"I'm due to run another patch through in a couple weeks or so," Donovan said. "I try to oil it once a month, but sometimes I forget."

"Well, you're a busy man. Thanks for your time, Ace."

Halliday returned the Henry, and the barber tucked it underneath his arm. "Glad I could help," he said. "I'll keep my ears open, and if you think of any other questions, stop by any time."

"Appreciate it," Halliday replied.

As they prepared to leave, Donovan spoke to Thorn for the first time. "A lucky break for you, last night."

"How's that?" Thorn asked.

"The shooter missing you."

"If it was accidental," he replied.

"You think he missed apurpose?"

"Won't know that until we find out who it was and ask him," Thorn replied.

"Well, if there's anything that I can do to end this bloody business, let me know," said Donovan.

Outside, Thorn turned to Halliday and asked, "What do you think?"

"His rifle has been cleaned since it was fired last, and it wasn't oiled last night."

"So scratch him off the list."

"Unless he's got another Henry I don't know about," said Halliday, "and some reason to want you dead."

"Which leaves the minister," Thorn said.

"Unless you want to check the Henry in my office first."

"I thought about it," Thorn admitted. "The arithmetic's all wrong."

"How's that?"

"You couldn't fire twice from the Lucky Strike, run back downstairs, and stash your rifle in the office rack in time to meet me in the street."

"Okay. Long as we trust each other."

"We don't know each other, Marshal. Not to speak of."

"Makes me feel better 'bout thinking for a minute you might be the moonlight killer."

"You'd be crazy if you hadn't wondered," Thorn replied.

"Guess I'm not crazy then," said Halliday. "Let's have a word with Silas French."

The predator believed in Jesus, once upon a time, but he no longer dotes on superstition. His experience in life has taught him better, made him recognize a pantheon of gods unknown to hidebound true believers in the "one true faith" of Europe, transported to the Americas and forced upon the native peoples there at gunpoint. He believes in *power* now, and recognizes it within himself.

That said, he still feels latent twinges now and then, the stirrings of his old life in the days before he was transformed into *Yenaldooshi*, the skinwalker. Today, in broad daylight, it draws him to a house of worship still familiar from his childhood, where he wasted countless hours lost in prayer to plaster figurines.

The Church of Saint Francis de Paula serves Tularosa's Roman Catholics, led by Father Luke Iglesias. It is constructed in the Spanish mission style so common in the former holdings of New Spain, truncated and absorbed by the United States during the latter 1840s. In accordance with the Territory's new tradition, it holds separate masses for white Catholics and those of Mexican descent, but neither has a service scheduled for this Monday morning. Stepping through its double doors, beneath the tower with its three bells hung beneath a cross, the predator has Saint Francis de Paula to himself.

Except, of course, for Father Luke.

The priest finds him before he can decide exactly why he's come. Vague yearning, or a haunting memory, has sparked a tingling in his chest the predator equates with human guilt. He is an alien to that sensation now, but recognizes that it once controlled his life, making him bow and scrape before the symbols of authority that never helped him in the least but only took his time and money, promising ephemeral rewards in Heaven after he was dead.

It all seems foolish now, and yet...

"May I help you, my son?" the priest inquires.

"I'm not sure," says the predator.

This all feels wrong to him—daylight, and no full moon

awaiting when the sun goes down—but he is in the grip of a compulsion and it will not be denied.

"You seem troubled," says Father Luke.

"I may be."

"Can't you tell?"

"It's...difficult."

The priest frowns. Says, "I should ask whether you're a Catholic."

"I was."

"But no longer? You've lapsed?"

"I've found another way."

"Perhaps that's what is troubling you."

The predator has no response to that. It's possible, but hardly in the way the *padre* seems to think.

"You *were* baptized?" asks Father Luke.

"A long, long time ago."

"Time is irrelevant. Perhaps if you were willing to confess..."

The notion almost makes him laugh aloud. He stifles that and says, "There's so much. Where would I begin?"

"In the confessional, my son. If you'll just follow me..."

He tags along, sniffing the air. Aside from incense in the sanctuary, he smells garlic on the priest's breath, wine, the tang of a cigar. Hardly abstemious, standing aloof from worldly things.

He recognizes the confessional, a standard type, with two doors behind curtains. Father Luke enters the left-hand cubicle, leaving the predator to take the right. He enters, sits, and Father Luke draws back a thin wooden partition, leaving crosshatched screen between them.

"Please proceed, my son."

The words come back to him as if by magic, dredged up from the swamp of his subconscious. Omitting the petition for forgiveness, he declares, "It has been twelve years since my last confession. I've abandoned your god in the service of the spirits that surround us all."

"Stop! If you don't believe—"

"I've offered sacrifices to the spirits of the Earth and Sky."

"When you say 'sacrifices'—"

"Eighteen sacrifices, Father. Two remain before I am transformed."

"Dear God! You don't mean—"

"I am *Yenaldooshi*. Tremble at my name."

He feels the change beginning, how incredible without the full moon overhead to bring it on. He lunges forward, smashing through the flimsy screen to reach for Father Luke, his talon-hands grasping the *padre*'s throat before he has a chance to scream.

"I own a Henry rifle, yes," said Silas French. "You know that, Marshal."

They were standing in the Free Will Baptist Church, a rainbow streaming through the stained-glass window set above the altar, catching sunlight from outside. Without it, Thorn surmised the chapel would have been a gloomy place, even with lanterns lighted on its walls. He counted ten long pews, divided by a central aisle, and wondered how many were filled for Sunday services.

"I'm asking, Reverend," said Marshal Halliday, "because somebody used a Henry when they fired at Mr. Thorn last night."

"And you suspect *me*?"

"It's a mere formality," the lawman said. "I have to

check the Henrys that I know about and make sure none of them were used."

"*You* have a Henry rifle, Marshal."

"Yes, I do. It's being checked as well."

"By whom?"

"That would be me," Thorn said.

"Ah, yes. The stranger in our midst, Mr. ...?"

"Gideon Thorn."

The preacher didn't offer to shake hands. Thorn was relieved, imagining the dry clutch of a lizard's paw.

"You find us in our hour of darkness, Mr. Thorn. One might say *in extremis.*"

At the point of death that was, in Latin.

"Your chapel was vandalized, I understand," said Thorn.

"The House of God was *desecrated,*" French corrected him. "I had to fast and pray for cleansing."

"And succeeded?"

"With the power of God, all things are possible."

"I know we've covered this, Pastor," said Halliday, "but if you've thought of anyone who'd wish you harm or hold a grudge against the church..."

"All sinners hate the word of God until they're saved and brought into the light," said French. "It is the nature of our curse from Eden to the present day. After the desecration, certain members of my flock withdrew. I won't say that they lost their faith, but they lacked moral fortitude to stand against the evil from without."

"You're still convinced it's an outsider, then?" the marshal asked.

"A stranger to the faith of Christ, at least," said French, his face carved in a scowl. Thorn pegged him as a frowning man and wondered if he ever smiled.

"So, not a *stranger* in the normal sense," said Halliday.

"You might ask so-called 'Father Luke'," French said.

"Why's that?" asked Halliday.

"Because Catholicism masks a sink of heresy! They practice rank idolatry and even tamper with the Ten Commandments to conceal their sin. Have you compared their so-called bible to the King James Version, either of you?"

"Sorry, no," said Halliday. Thorn held his tongue.

"They drop the abjuration against graven images entirely—that's original Commandment number two—and move up number three to take its place, which bans taking the name of God in vain. To make the final count match up, they split the Tenth Commandment into two, dividing coveting thy neighbor's wife from coveting his worldly goods. Can you imagine the audacity?"

"I'll check that out," the marshal said.

"It's only the beginning," French pressed on. "Throughout their altered bible there are nine books absent from King James. Their Pentateuch has *seven* books, if you can fathom that. For Heaven's sake, the very name itself means *five*!"

"You have some reason to believe that Father Luke's involved in what's been going on around the village?" Thorn inquired.

"Strange practices," French answered back. "Who launched the Inquisition with its torture and rapine? Who keeps a list of human beings tagged as 'saints'? I'll say no more!"

"About that Henry rifle..."

"It's at home," French said. "I have no need of it in church, where God protects his worshipers."

Thorn almost said, *Except for stray arms on the altar,* but he kept it to himself. He glanced at Halliday, was on the verge of shrugging when a bell began to toll at the far end of Tularosa.

"Well, speak of the Devil!" French spat out.

"We'll leave you now, Pastor," said Halliday. "But I'll be by to check that rifle."

"As you wish, Marshal."

They reached the thoroughfare. The single bell continued its monotonous *ding-dong*.

"Time for a service?" Thorn inquired.

"Not on a Monday, and they ring all three for Mass."

"So check it out?"

"I think we'd better," Halliday replied, and set off down the street.

TWELVE

CHURCH OF SAINT FRANCIS DE PAULA

"Jesus!" Heck Halliday walked once around the dangling corpse, skirting the pool of blood and offal spread beneath it, and returned to stand beside Gideon Thorn.

Father Luke Iglesias had died the hard way, although Thorn could not decide exactly what had killed him. With his purple face, the church's central bell rope tied around his neck, feet dangling a good twelve inches off the floor, he might have died from hanging. On the other hand, someone had ripped open his abdomen between the *padre*'s sternum and his groin, spilling a heap of his internal organs down his cassock to the blood-soaked floor.

The stain and heaping of his innards made it clear the priest was gutted *after* he was hanged, but had it happened rapidly enough to snuff his life before the rope cut off his wind and circulation to his brain? Beyond that, when Thorn took a closer look, he saw the damage to the priest's face and his neck beneath the noose, more blood soaked through his backwards collar and the upper portion of his cassock.

"Someone wanted to make damn sure he was dead," said Halliday, then suddenly remembered where he was and muttered "Sorry" with his eyes turned toward the ceiling.

Thorn, tempted to tell him there was no one listening, decided not to speak.

Behind them, in the street outside the church, a gaping crowd had gathered, members straining for a peek into the shadows, through the open double doors. Some on them had been on the scene when Thorn and Halliday arrived, the marshal barking at them to remain outside and spare the scene until it was examined.

Not that they were learning much so far.

Father Iglesias had been attacked in the confessional— or *through* it, from the evidence available. Thorn wasn't Catholic but knew the way it worked. The priest sat on one side, a penitent directly opposite and separated from him by a screen that offered some small modicum of privacy. That didn't mean the one confessing was unknown, unrecognized, but in the absence of a living witness to the murder, he remained anonymous.

Whoever came to call, the killer had progressed from spilling secrets to a brutal smashing through the flimsy barrier between him and the priest. Blood in the cubicle and on the church floor, leading to the spot where Father Luke was hanged, proved that the priest was injured, maybe dead or dying, by the time the bell rope cinched around his neck. The hanging had involved lifting his body —no small feat, since Father Luke had weighed at least one hundred sixty pounds, worse yet if he was still alive and struggling—to string him up and leave him dangling.

"What about that noose?" asked Halliday.

"It took some time," Thorn said.

Indeed, the bell rope was not simply tied around the priest's neck. Prior to hanging Father Luke, the murderer had tied a proper hangman's noose at the end, seven turns to the rope with a slipknot to cinch it and bear the man's weight.

"I've tied a few of those myself," said Halliday. "Takes me about five minutes, give or take."

"So Father Luke was either dead or past resisting when it went around his neck."

"Hoisting the man one-handed, slipping that over his head." Halliday scowled. "That took some strength."

"Maybe enough to tear some other victims limb from limb," Thorn said.

"Same killer then, you think?" the marshal asked him.

"Do you doubt it?" Thorn replied.

"I *hope* we don't have two, but this kill changes everything."

Thorn nodded. "Daylight, with the town awake. The hanging, and the mutilation's not the same."

Halliday leaned in closer to the priest, then backed away and shook his head. "I can't tell if his heart's been taken."

Thorn already knew it wasn't with the other organs lying on the floor. "The undertaker can report on that."

And, no surprise, Josiah Groom was standing in the doorway now, his shadow spilling from the threshold almost to the spot where Thorn and Halliday stood with the corpse. The undertaker held his hat in front of him, face long and grim beneath his graying, middle-parted hair. Beside him, burdened with his camera gear, stood Myron Colfax from the *Tularosa Trumpet*.

"Marshal?" Colfax called into the church. "Do you need photographs before the body is removed?"

Halliday muttered something Thorn's ears didn't catch, then called back toward the doorway, "Myron, you and Mr. Groom come in. Nobody else!"

The corpse had been removed to Groom's establishment, four of the gawkers volunteering for that task, most of the others trailing them along the thoroughfare, down to the mortuary. Halliday and Thorn retreated to the marshal's office, ducked inside and shut the door behind them. Halliday collapsed behind his desk and waved Thorn toward one of the two remaining chairs.

"This does for me," he said, resignedly. "I won't be reelected after this. In fact, I may as well turn in my badge right now."

"I haven't known you long," Thorn said, "but you don't strike me as a quitter."

"I'm not, most of the time. But *this*—" He made a vague, expansive gesture, taking in the room, the town, the world at large. "I can't bounce back from this. The other killings, going on at night and mostly outside town, were one thing. Horrible, but little I could do about them, being mostly in the county sheriff's jurisdiction. Now the bastard's struck three times in Tularosa proper, this time in broad daylight, in a goddamn church for Chrissakes! Would you reelect a lawman who let that go on?"

"I like to think I'd realize he wasn't prescient and vote on how he dealt with crimes after they happened. No one's claiming you can see the future, Marshal."

"No? I wouldn't like to poll that crowd out there, right now."

"The cure for your dilemma is to catch the killer."

"Sure thing," Halliday responded, almost snorting. "Just like that, with nineteen people murdered and his pattern shot to hell."

"And that could be the key," Thorn said. "Daylight, the full moon past, his choice of target. What would draw him to that church and make him kill the priest?"

"Last time he went to church," said Halliday, "he left poor Myron's arm at Free Will Baptist. Maybe he just hates religion?"

"But for this attack, as you've already pointed out, he threw his pattern out the window. This was *special* to him somehow. Solve that riddle, and you'll have your man."

Before Heck could consider that, the office door burst open and a stocky man barged in, red-faced and dusty from the trail, a well-worn Stetson planted squarely on his head. Halliday thought that style of hat was called "Boss of the Plains," and this one wore it as if he believed the name was meant for him alone.

"So *here* you are," he said, by way of greeting. "Were you going to inform me, Marshal?"

"About what?"

Stant glowered at him, moving closer to Halliday's desk. "About the savage death of Tularosa's minister. What else?"

"First off," Heck said, "he's not—*wasn't*—our only minister. There's also Pastor French."

"A raving bigot! Why, he's not—"

"And *second,* I wasn't aware you needed special notice anytime someone gets killed."

"I attend his church!" the new arrival snarled through gritted teeth. "I dare say, from the look of those I see at Mass, that I'm the primary supporter of Saint Francis de Paula."

"And you clearly got the word straight off, arriving now before the body's even cold."

"As luck would have it, I was on my way to—"

"How's your boy?" Heck interrupted him again.

"Declan? He's fine, Marshal. What has he got to do with anything?"

So this was Jubal Stant, Thorn realized, the young drunk's father from the Lucky Strike.

"Just passing time, Jubal. I hear a couple of your riders had to pick him up on Saturday, when he got pitched out of the tavern. Drunk at the noon hour, someone said."

"He had a small lapse, but that's none of your concern. You know his issues. What I want from you, right now, is how you plan on dealing with these heinous crimes."

"I've got a man headed for Alamogordo, letting Sheriff Rooney know what's happening. I'm also thinking maybe we should ask the army for some help."

"The army?"

"Camp Concordia, outside El Paso," Halliday replied.

"But that's over a hundred miles away!"

"More reason to get started, soon as I can find another deputy."

"And in the meantime?" Stant demanded.

"I'll be following whatever leads develop from the latest scene," Halliday said. And added, for the hell of it, "Working with Mr. Thorn."

"I don't know who that is," Stand fumed.

"Gideon Thorn," the man in black spoke up. "We haven't met."

"Are you some kind of law enforcement officer?" Stant challenged him.

Halliday butted in. "Thorn has experience with things like this," he said. "That's all you need to know, Jubal."

"Experience!" Stant fairly spat the word. "Some of us aren't content to sit and wait, Marshal."

"Meaning your riders, when you give the word to start a manhunt?"

"And whoever else rides with us."

"I'd advise you against any vigilante action," Halliday declared. "It's criminal. You know it, I know it, and so does Sheriff Rooney."

"*You* advise *me*?" Stant's red face split into a ferocious grin. "No, Marshal, *I'm* advising *you*. If you can't do your job, the rest of us will do it for you and elect a fit replacement in November."

"Just mind what I say, Jubal. You or your cronies harm someone, I'm coming after you."

"I'm safe then, since it's obvious you can't catch anyone!"

Stant turned and left the office, slammed the door behind him, and was gone.

"He's not a friend, I take it," Thorn observed.

Halliday sighed and leaned back in his chair. "Jubal's the single biggest rancher in this section of Otero County, running cattle. Catholic, you may have gathered. Proud supporter of the church, and wants to make sure everybody knows it."

"What was that about his son's 'issues'?" Thorn asked.

"Now that's a sad story," said Halliday. "Declan was four years old when he was captured by a hostile raiding party, Navajos, back in the spring of 1860. Jubal spent the next three years trying to find him, never coming close. The cavalry recovered him in '63, after they hit a village in Socorro County. Brought him back to Jubal, but he's never been the same. Grew up all right—bigger then you are, now —but still. The redskins got inside his head those years they had him, raisin' him, if you can call it that. He drinks to blot it out, I think. Jubal tries keeping him away from liquor, but the boy goes his own way."

"That's hard," Thorn said.

"About the worst thing that a father can imagine. Might've been a mercy if the Navajos had killed him."

Getting off that morbid train of thought, Thorn asked Halliday, "Were you serious about the army?"

"Damn right. Sheriff Rooney's fine at chasing rustlers, the odd robber, but he can't keep up with this crap. As for me...well, here I sit."

"You have someone in mind to carry word?"

"Steve Decker, works part-time around the livery."

"Decker? Is he related to—?"

"Dead Myron's younger brother, turned eighteen in January. He's been itching for a chance to make things right. I've put him off till now, out of consideration for his mother, but a ride to Camp Concordia seems safe enough."

"You think the cavalry will get involved?" asked Thorn.

The marshal shrugged. "Depends on how the colonel feels on any given day, I guess, and what else he's involved in. Sends his men out chasing Indians from time to time, without much luck. If anyone can sell him on it, I'd say Steve's the one. The personal approach."

Thorn wasn't sure that troops would help their cause, but he could understand Halliday's bind. With no real leads, he still had to *appear* engaged and searching for the killer, or he'd soon have a rebellion on his hands.

"I'll leave you to it then," he said, and rose to go. "You've got your hands full now."

Halliday raised those hands, waggling the fingers. Said, "And I can't catch a goddamn thing."

"Ah, Mr. Thorn!"

He recognized the voice and turned to face the *Tularosa Trumpet*'s editor. "All finished with the photos, Mr. Colfax?"

"Working on Wednesday's issue," Colfax said. "Between the shepherds and Father Iglesias, I may be adding on an extra page."

"Well, I won't keep you any longer."

"Heading for the Lucky Strike perhaps?"

"I am," Thorn granted.

"I'd still like to finish up that interview," said Colfax, keeping pace with him. "A human interest item, as we say, to take the edge off blood and gore."

"Well..."

"I'm determined, Mr. Thorn. Dinner's on me!"

Thorn mulled it over for a second, then he nodded. "It's a deal. But I'm not going into any further detail on my family."

"Of course, of course. I understand completely."

What the newsman *didn't* understand was Thorn's shortage of knowledge on the subject. Other than the fragments of his memory, he knew no more about the massacre that claimed his parents and his brother than did Colfax, pleading for his time.

They got a window table at the Lucky Strike and spent a moment with the standard menu. Thorn ordered the *enchiladas con chili rojo,* with rice and refried beans, while Colfax picked the pan-fried trout with baked potato and a side of collard greens. After the waitress poured their coffee, Colfax placed his notebook on the table and began.

"Without encroaching on the details of your loss," he said, "can you allude however briefly to your private tragedy?"

"There nothing more to say," Thorn told him. "As I told you earlier, we lived in Kansas Territory—Colorado Territory now—along the east slope of the Rockies. In November 1854 something attacked the cabin, killed my folks, and left me with this mark—" bowing his head to show the streak of white—"as a reminder."

"Terrible!" said Colfax, scribbling hastily. "When you say 'something'..."

"As I explained before," Thorn said, "I haven't got a clue. Bear-sized at least, from my perspective as a child. All teeth and claws."

"But you escaped."

"A fluke."

"Fortuitous indeed. And in November! Was it snowing?"

"Yes. Somebody found me wandering. I'm still not clear on who or how."

"And after that?"

"I wound up in an orphanage at Lawrence."

"Scene of Quantrill's bloody raid in 1863?"

"The very same. But I was gone by then, of course."

"Remarkable! And where, exactly, did you go?"

"My father's sister got wind of the incident in Boston and she sent for me." He absolutely was not mentioning Obi Magoro or the details of their interaction over time.

"Boston, you say?"

"She was the last Thorn on the bush, except for me."

"And had the wherewithal to take you in?"

"Correct." If Colfax wanted to know more about the Thorn fortune, he could research it for himself.

"And so you went to Harvard."

"Yes." More ground now trodden twice.

"My word! And yet ... well ... here you are."

"You mean in Tularosa?"

"In the West, at large," Colfax replied. "Searching for legends, is it?"

"No, sir. Legends date back into ancient history. The Greeks, Romans, whomever. I'm concerned about things happening—or *said* to happen—in the West right now, today."

"Like Tularosa's murders."

Thorn was nodding when the waitress brought their plates. He took a bite of enchilada, found it filled with shredded beef, onions and cheese, the chili sauce delectable. Colfax attacked his trout but kept his thoughts on track.

"If I may ask, sir, how many cases have you actively investigated?"

Thorn forked down some beans and rice, running the silent count. "This makes my fifth," he said. "They aren't all crimes, per se."

"And did you solve the others?"

"To my satisfaction, yes. Some sprang from rumors, unsupported. Others were more...substantial."

"And in Tularosa's case? Do you feel optimistic after the events occurring since you came to town?"

"First thing to bear in mind," Thorn said, "I'm not a lawman. I have no plan or intention to obstruct local authorities in any way. I have no powers of arrest beyond those held by any other citizen."

"That being said..."

"I am in no sense an official and do not perform in that capacity at any time."

"Yet you still hope to solve the crimes?"

"I hope to learn the truth, both here and in a broader sense."

"That's quite mysterious," Colfax replied.

"Is it?" Thorn shrugged. "You'd best make something up then. It's the best that I can do."

And having said that, focused on his meal.

THIRTEEN

SOUTH OF TULAROSA: JUNE 21, 1875

Steve Decker was relieved to have a job at last, not sweeping out the livery, but doing something finally to catch his brother's murderer. Given a choice, he rather would have met the bastard face to face, a showdown in the grand old Western style, but if he told the truth, that prospect scared him half to death.

Steve wasn't much for fighting, never had been, and it nagged him now, the way Myron had taken care of him after their father died from snakebite, with his leg swollen so big it wouldn't fit his trouser leg and Mama had to slit it up the inseam. Steve was grateful for the help his brother gave him, absolutely, but it riled him, too. Made him feel weak and insignificant compared to Myron, bringing home the bacon for their family from any job, finally putting on a badge to keep the village safe.

That hadn't lasted long, and when the killer came for Myron, that was like one last slap in the face for Steve. He'd dreamed for years of growing up, acquiring skills, reaching a place where he could pay Steve back for everything, and suddenly, just on the verge of getting there, the opportunity was snatched away from him.

Okay, too late. But now *he* wore the badge, if only temporarily, and he was heading southward toward El Paso —more specifically to Camp Concordia, outside the city— on a chestnut gelding borrowed from the livery. He wore his brother's pistol strapped around his waist and carried food enough for two nights on the trail, together with a full canteen, a coil of rope, and bedding.

What else did he need, except the grit to pull it off?

The note from Marshal Halliday was tucked into his shirt pocket, worded the best that Heck could manage to persuade a colonel that his help was both required and justified under the law. Steve knew there were restrictions on the use of U.S. troops to aid civilian lawmen, dicey in those days with Reconstruction winding down and everyone below the Mason-Dixon Line inflamed by how that power had been used—or not used, in some cases—for the relief of former slaves.

Steve didn't know that much about the Civil War, except he thought that slavery was wrong, imagining himself in chains and forced to work for nothing, but his focus was the task at hand, getting the message through, pursuing vengeance for his brother.

Halliday was late approaching him, with better than a hundred miles to ride before Steve reached the army base, but Decker hadn't put it off till morning. He had barely sworn the oath to execute his duties faithfully—well, the *one* duty, all he had—when he was packing up, kissing his mother on the cheek, and riding hell-for-leather in a race against sundown. He had only covered fifteen miles or so when dusk began to fall across the desert, and he'd have to find a decent campsite soon, before full night surrounded him.

It wouldn't be *too* dark, of course, not with a waning gibbous moon three nights past full. That made him think about the Mexicans who'd died on Friday night—which, in its turn, reminded him of Myron, back in March. Not that the image of his brother's ravaged, partial body ever truly left Steve's waking mind.

In other circumstances, Decker would have thought that he was safe out on the range, but Father Luke's murder in church that very afternoon scotched any such idea. If sudden death could strike in daylight, in the very heart of Tularosa, that told Steve no one was safe.

With purple shadows stretching out around him, he began to seek a campsite and discovered one with running water, just a small spring, but its output was clear and better than nothing. Enough pale grass was sprouting for the chestnut to get by on, and he scrounged some dead wood for his small campfire. He checked around for snakes, then spread his blanket on the ground and opened up a can of pork and beans.

Sparse fare, but it would do.

And when he went to sleep, if he could manage it, he'd keep his brother's pistol close.

TULAROSA

After he left Colfax to settle up their dinner bill, Gideon Thorn embarked on a slow walking tour of the village, making sure that he was visible. He had no reason to believe his would-be killer from the night before would try again, but just in case, he wanted to allow the shooter ample opportunity to make a move. It was the best way Thorn could think of—no, make that the *only* way—to draw his adversary out and place the two of them on level ground.

And even then he had to ask himself: how crazy *was* the moonlight killer, after all?

Crazy enough to break the pattern that had served him well for sixteen months, and while he'd got away with it in the short term, it might come back to bite him yet.

Thorn mulled over that pattern, broken twice within a day's time, trying to make sense of it. The shots fired into his hotel room didn't take much thought, a case of panic on the killer's part, trying to take Thorn out or scare him off the case. And yet, despite that miss and the abortive chase that followed, coming nowhere close to apprehension, he'd returned at high noon to kill Father Luke inside his church, where stray parishioners might drop in any time and catch him in the act.

What drew the killer to Saint Francis de Paula with murder in mind? If he was Catholic, had he said something in confession that came back to haunt him? Had he silenced Father Luke to save himself? While not affiliated with the Church of Rome or any other sect per se, Thorn understood the workings of confession and its other rituals. Under the Sacrament of Penance, priests were absolutely barred from airing anything they heard in the confessional, for any reason, under any circumstance, including threats of death directed at the priest or any other person. In the case of crimes anticipated or ongoing, priests were granted power to *encourage* the confessee to surrender, but they could not order it or share their secret information with police, and no process of law could force them to.

Of course, a Catholic would know that, ought to feel secure, but in a case like Tularosa's, where the murderer was almost certainly insane, logic played little part. And now that Father Luke had been removed as an imagined threat, if such he was, what happened next? Would the moonlight assassin now revert to his old method, striking once a month in perpetuity until he was discovered by some other means and brought to book? Would he depart from fear of being linked to the priest's murder through their church?

It irritated Thorn that he had no idea, but he had gotten used to the uncertainty since leaving Boston for his rambling tour of the West, pursuing mysteries. Some proved to be ridiculously easy when subjected to his scrutiny; others held secrets he might never solve.

In which case, how was he to learn the truth about his family?

Was everything he did a glaring waste of time?

Not yet, he thought, and tipped his hat in silent greeting to a pair of ladies hurrying toward their respective homes. Neither responded with a smile, though one of them acknowledged him with a distracted nod.

The homicides were sapping Tularosa's strength to carry on as a community. At this point, neighbor lived in fear of neighbor, and that curse might soon extend to families, driving its wedge between people who had been close since birth. Thorn cursed his inability to make it stop at once, but moved on with renewed determination to remain at least a little longer—long enough to find out if the killer would continue deviating from his "norm" and thus making himself more vulnerable.

Grim-faced, Gideon began his walk back to the Tularosa House and what he feared would be a fitful sleep.

SOUTH OF TULAROSA

The predator experiences a delightful sense of freedom that he's never felt before. Although he's still bound to the moon, he realizes now that his transcendence has proceeded to the point where he can act by will alone, without slavish devotion to a pale orb in the nighttime sky. If he desires to strike on other nights, or even in the daylight, he is fully capable.

One thing he is *not* sure of: does the death of Father Luke count toward his twenty sacrifices, mandatory to achieve full independence for himself? He reckons it should not, being impulsive and conducted without full changeover to his beastly form. There must be *rules*, of course, or what's the use of any ritual?

Tonight, again, he's hunting without sanction from his Mother Moon, three nights beyond its full and no longer commanding him to feed. His current task is a necessity, to stop the solitary rider from approaching Camp Concordia and seeking military aid. The last thing he, the predator, needs is a troop of soldiers bivouacked in Tularosa, watching who goes where, inquiring when and why.

One death can solve that problem for the moment. By the time another deputy is found to try again, with any luck, another full moon will arrive and he can find a pair of victims to complete his rite of passage into immortality.

Perhaps he'll even sacrifice his Master next time, putting paid to the old man's incessant meddling and complaints. That prospect thrills the predator but it will have to wait. The old man is a prize to savor at the end of his becoming, not a bone to gnaw and toss away at whim. If he had any other kin they could be added to the list, but there are just the two of them. The line dies with his Master and a new breed starts with him.

His destiny is written in the midnight sky.

Tonight he rides his buckskin stallion, since he will not change until the final moment of attack. He has miles to traverse, and he cannot pursue a mounted rider on his own two feet—or four, for that matter. He will overtake the messenger in conventional style, then test his power to transform without a full moon overhead.

And failing that, he has his Henry rifle in its saddle boot.

Whatever way you slice it, dead is dead.

Dusk catches up to him and fills the predator with strength. He is a creature of the night, emboldened by the darkness and the stars above, an avid audience that watches him perform. Invincible on nights of the full moon, he is not sure if that will translate to another night before his final transmutation, and he will proceed with caution on this hunt—or, anyhow, as far as he is able to restrain himself. Beyond that, when he smells blood, tastes it, he may not possess the willpower to stop.

It might be best, he strategizes, for the messenger to simply disappear. Leave Tularosa wondering if he got through or showed a yellow streak and kept on riding, glad to flee the village and abandon his responsibility. If that's not feasible, the predator will mangle him to a degree that shocks the populace, whenever they send someone out to look for him, and make them realize that there is no escape. No weapon and no variation of a uniform can cage the predator once he attains full strength.

The shamans have decreed it, and he's never known them to be wrong.

At last, with full night coming on, he sees a spark on the

horizon, growing as he closes in to finally become the flicker of a campfire. It may prove to be some idle traveler, a hapless pilgrim drifting, but the predator intuits that his chosen prey is hunched beside that fire, warming himself, perhaps consuming something that will fatten him and make the final feast more pleasant.

Not that blood and raw manflesh have ever disappointed him.

He slows the buckskin stallion to a trot, then to a walk. At last, with something like a half-mile left to go, the predator dismounts and leads his horse by hand toward his appointment with the messenger. It is a fitting twist, he thinks that Marshal Halliday has chosen Myron Decker's younger brother for the task.

The predator enjoys an opportunity to keep it in the family.

Steve Decker finished off his can of pork and beans, scraping the bottom with his spoon so that he got it all and none escaped. He licked the spoon and dried it on his jeans, considered burying the empty can, but finally decided not to bother, casting it aside into the sagebrush. What was one stray can in a territory spanning more than one hundred twenty thousand square miles?

His chestnut gelding whickered in the dark, not agitated by the sound of it, but Decker still responded as if somebody had walked over his grave, a shudder slipping down his spine. He pulled his late brother's Colt Model 1861 Navy revolver and set the weapon in his lap, hand resting on its curved butt with the walnut grips, their shine long faded from excessive handling.

Myron had bought the pistol second-hand, its vendor telling him some tale about its use during the Civil War, in the battles at Fort Henry and at Hampton Roads. Steve didn't have a clue if that was true or not and didn't care. He'd fired the pistol, knew that he could hit a target with it six or eight times out of ten, and that was all that mattered now.

Too bad his brother hadn't thought to cock and fire it on the night he died. The Tularosa murders might have ended then and there, although some wags insisted that preceding victims had been armed and shooting when the killer—man, beast, whatever in hell it was—ripped into them.

Steve Decker wouldn't be mistaken for a hero, but he had a score to settle with his brother's murderer and hoped that he would have the chance, although the prospect also chilled him with an icy pang of fear.

What would his mother do if he were killed like Myron, leaving her alone? Steve liked to think that other Tularosans would look out for her but knew damn well he couldn't count on it. The town was small, but still infected with the malady of each man for himself and Devil take the hindmost in the end.

In that respect, at least, it was the same as any other village, town, or city in the world.

The answer was to come back safe and sound. Steve knew that much and kept the Navy Colt close by as he spread out his bedroll and lay down, his saddlebags doubling as an uncomfortable pillow. If he slept at all, and that was dodgy, he expected to be waking up throughout the night ahead, listening to the prairie sounds and trembling underneath his blanket.

Trust the fire, he thought, *to keep the scavengers at bay.*

And if that didn't work, be ready with the pistol.

Steve was surprised when he woke up, after some unknown interval, and blinked skyward to find the moon and stars had moved about on him, marking the passage of an hour, maybe more. He lay still for a moment, listening for whatever had wakened him, uncertain whether it had been a noise or an unsettled dream. At last his ears picked out the sound of something circling at the outer edge of failing firelight and he sat up, squinting into darkness.

Nothing. And he wondered for another second why that should disturb him, then he understood.

His horse was gone.

He must have heard the chestnut gelding as it fled the camp—but no. If that were true, why did he *still* hear something moving stealthily around him in the dark?

Steve threw his blanket back, struggled to rise, and cocked his pistol, turning slowly as his ears followed the sound. His campfire had burned down to glowing coals, but he had dead wood lying near and tossed a few more sticks onto the embers, waiting while they caught and flared. Fresh light pushed back the shadows, but he still saw nothing to accompany the circling noise.

But wait. Was that a low-pitched *growl*?

Some kind of animal, it had to be. A lone coyote possibly, or more than one, if they were hunting as a pack tonight.

Steve knew they couldn't understand him, but he spoke up anyway. "Get out of here!" he shouted. "Scat! I'll blow your damn brains out!"

The only answer was another, louder growl.

He tried to fix it in the night, lifted the Navy Colt and braced himself before he squeezed the trigger, blinded for an instant by its muzzle flash, ears stinging from the shot. Steve half expected to hear animals scurry away, but no such luck. Instead, whatever had approached his camp stopped moving and unleashed a chilling sound some-where between a shriek and roar.

Behind him.

Steve was turning with his weapon when it struck him, knocked him flat, and pounced on top of him. He felt claws ripping at his back, too large for any desert dog he'd ever heard of, gouts of blood erupting from the long, deep wounds.

A scream stuck in his throat as something gripped his head and wrenched it right around, backwards, to face up at the stars.

FOURTEEN

TULAROSA: JUNE 22, 1875

Gideon Thorn came down to breakfast early at the Lucky Strike. He ordered *huevos divorciados*—fried eggs atop tortillas, refried beans and rice, with one egg doused in red sauce and the other one in green. With steaming coffee, it immediately cleared the final cobwebs from his brain and let him focus on the day ahead.

It looked like waiting, for the county sheriff to arrive and Halliday's young deputy to reach the army base at Camp Concordia, down on the Texas border. If the camp commander played along and didn't send the rider packing empty-handed, there'd be more time wasted while a small detail of soldiers readied for the trail, then they would have to ride the hundred miles and change back north to Tularosa, probably arriving sometime around noon tomorrow, Thursday.

Meanwhile, that Wednesday afternoon, Josiah Groom was burying the two shepherds on Tularosa's version of Boot Hill. Thorn hadn't yet decided whether he would dodge the ceremony or attend it. Having found the corpses, with Heck Halliday and others, he experienced a certain sense of obligation to the two dead strangers, but it only stretched so far.

Detachment was the key to probing unsolved crimes, but Thorn had yet to master it completely.

He was halfway through his meal, enjoying it immensely, when a chestnut horse passed by, trotting along the thoroughfare alone, no tack or saddle on it, no one in attendance. That struck Thorn as strange, but not enough to make him leave his breakfast, even though a pair of merchants on the sidewalk opposite were pointing at the animal, one of them ducking back inside his shop to call for someone else. The other crossed behind the horse, jogging, and passed from sight in the direction of the marshal's office.

Gideon had not been present when Halliday's deputy rode out to Camp Concordia, therefore he did not recognize the borrowed horse returning riderless. His curiosity increased as the first merchant he had seen emerged with yet another man in tow, perhaps his clerk, and started jabbering, nodding in the direction of the livery.

Disturbed, Thorn took a spare tortilla from his plate and started pushing food onto his fork, devouring it as rapidly as possible. He had a vague uneasy feeling now, something amiss, and finished mopping up his meal as Marshal Halliday appeared, trailed by the storekeeper who'd gone to fetch him, both men following the horse along the thoroughfare.

Thorn left his nearly empty plate with money on the folded napkin, donned his hat, and went outside to join the short parade. By then, a few more shop workers had spied the horse and people tracking it, lining the wooden sidewalks to observe what happened next. There was no easy banter, no loud calling back and forth, only watching with an expectant sense of gloom.

Heck Halliday was talking to the hostler at the livery when Thorn caught up, the hostler nodding, telling him, "Yessir. That there's the gelding Steve borrowed to run your errand yesterday."

The full weight of it settled on Thorn's shoulders then. A missing deputy, and nothing to suggest he'd simply fallen off his horse, since it had come back without any trace of saddle or the other gear required for riding. Thorn found it more likely that the rider and his animal had been in camp last night, when the chestnut escaped—but what had spooked it? And why wasn't it secured somehow?

As if in answer to his silent inquiry, the hostler pointed, telling Halliday, "See there, Marshal? Part of a hobble Decker musta used to tie it. Notice where it's been cut through, as clean as anything."

Thorn saw a loop of rawhide hanging loosely from the gelding's left-front fetlock, sliced close to the leg, with the remainder of the hobble missing. That confirmed his sense that it had managed to escape from camp, but with a twist: the animal had been deliberately freed.

By whom? Why would the deputy release his animal and stay afoot? Would an attacker take the time or trouble to cut through the gelding's bonds?

Halliday noticed Thorn and asked, "You heard?"

"Your deputy's," Thorn said. "Cut loose."

"Goddamn it!" flared the marshal. "Why would Steve do that?"

"Don't make no sense," the hostler said. "No sense at all."

"And now I have to go out looking for him," Halliday

told no one in particular. To Thorn he said, "You wanna come along?"

Thorn nodded. Said, "I wouldn't miss it for the world."

Shadow was glad to be out of the livery, as comfortable as it was. The stallion liked to be in motion, traveling, and Thorn just had to point it, then hang on. Halliday rode a lemon-silla mare, galloping south along the road they figured Decker must have taken on his way to Camp Concordia. Nobody else from town had volunteered to ride along, which came as no surprise to Thorn.

The killer—if he was responsible for Decker's disappearance—had abandoned any semblance of the pattern from his other crimes. Assuming Decker had been set upon in camp, that meant another night attack, but well beyond the full moon murders Tularosans had been educated to expect. The message now: in town or out, daylight or dark, lawman or otherwise, no one was safe.

It was a recipe for panic in the village and beyond.

"I should've called on someone else," said Halliday, when they slowed down to walk their animals a while.

"It would have turned out just the same," Thorn said.

"But then, there wouldn't only be one Decker left. Their mother wouldn't be alone."

The woman had appeared before they left the livery, alerted at her home by someone, weeping silently as she passed Halliday to stroke the chestnut gelding. She'd said nothing after that, but turned accusing eyes on Halliday before she left, a couple of the town's women guiding her back to wherever she had come from.

"After Myron," Halliday opined, "I wouldn't think that Steve would let himself be taken by surprise."

"We still don't know what happened," Thorn reminded him.

"I know. But I can feel it in my gut."

"Let's wait and see."

Another thirty minutes passed before they found the campsite, wisps of smoke still rising from the ashes of its fire. The rest all looked familiar from the shepherd's camp they had discovered yesterday, but only one man had been mauled and disemboweled this time.

"There's something off about his head," said Halliday.

"It's facing backwards," Thorn observed. "His neck's been broken."

"Christ all Friday. Maybe that's a mercy, anyhow."

Thorn wasn't spotting any signs of mercy at the murder scene. Long gashes marked Steve Decker's back, had bled profusely, with a portion of his spine bared, and it seemed as if his organs had been ripped out through the back somehow, along his waistline. At some point, the murderer had spent time breaking Decker's knee and elbow joints, freeing the lower limbs to point in weird directions nature never had intended. The effect, viewed as a whole, reminded Thorn of some demented artwork.

"Time went into this," said Halliday.

Ignoring that, Thorn said, "The killer had to follow him from town, or at the very least to head him off."

"Which means he knew I'd sent Steve."

"Well, sent *someone*, anyway."

"Cutting us off from help."

"Preventing contact with the army, when you also sent a man to fetch the sheriff."

"Adam Rooney's in the same position I am," Halliday replied. "We've both been chasing this son of a bitch for well over a year and getting nowhere."

"But the killer was afraid of soldiers coming in."

"More men," the marshal said. "And maybe more professional, although I wouldn't count on it."

"More eyes," said Thorn. "More armed patrols."

"You think he's still got something left to do in Tularosa?"

"Maybe. The only thing I'm sure of is that he rode here and had to ride away."

"So there'd be tracks," said Halliday.

"With any luck at all."

They found the hoof prints of a second horse and rider twenty minutes later, trailing Decker south from Tularosa. Halfway back to town, those tracks veered off from the road, leading away to the northeast. Halliday led Thorn in pursuit, six miles and then some, before slowing almost to a halt.

"The only thing out this way is the Stant spread," he told Gideon.

"Stant who was riled about the church where we found Father Luke?"

"The very same."

"Whose son was taken by the Navajo."

"None other," Halliday replied, dejectedly. "Looks like we need to have another word with him."

Outriders met them when they crossed some unseen boundary onto the Stant ranch, asking Halliday his business, then escorting them to meet the man in charge. The place where they wound up was built around a sprawling farmhouse, two stories in front, with single-story wings stretching away to north and south. Four chimneys sprouted from the roof, two of them trailing smoke. Around the house, Thorn saw a spacious barn, a bunkhouse for the hands, two privies, and assorted other outbuildings. Horses circled around inside a pair of twin corrals.

As they approached, one of their escorts fired a pistol shot into the air, and by the time they reached the house its owner had emerged onto the broad front porch, flanked by a pair of men with six-guns tied down low. Stant squinted at them from his Stetson's shade, wearing the same frown that he had displayed on Monday afternoon, at Halliday's office.

"You two come to join the hunting party?" Stant inquired, when they had closed to twenty yards.

"Tracking a killer on our own," Halliday answered back.

"The hell is that supposed to mean."

"I sent a man to Camp Concordia after we saw you yesterday," said Halliday.

"Admitting you can't handle it?"

"He camped out on the plain last night, and then his horse came back to town this morning. We just found him at his camp, like all the rest. The killer's tracks lead straight back here."

Stant blinked at that, then snapped, "Bullshit. You must've read the signs wrong."

"Grab a horse," said Halliday. "Come look at them yourself."

"Don't need to," Stant replied. "My men were all accounted for last night."

"You watched 'em sleeping, did you, Jubal?"

"You've got a frigging nerve, Marshal. Come on my land accusing honest men of murder. Or are you accusing *me*?"

Gideon Thorn knew they were sitting on a powder keg but still spoke up for the first time. "We'd like to have a few words with your son."

"You would, eh? I don't see you wearing any kind of badge Mister ... Thorn, was it?" Turning back toward Halliday, Stant asked, "He speak for you?"

"On this he does."

"Well isn't this a pile of crap. You know what Declan's been through, Halliday."

"Long time ago."

"A thing like that stays with you."

Halliday was nodding. "That's one reason why we need to see him."

"You and *this* one ride in here, inferring that my boy's done something criminal."

"The word's 'implying'," Thorn corrected him. "You made the inference."

"Smart bastard." Turning back to Halliday. "You want Declan, run back and get a warrant."

"Just some questions, Jubal," said the marshal.

"Screw your questions and screw both of you. The only thing you're doing here is holding up the hunt for whoever killed Father Luke and all them others."

"Is that your last word, Jubal?"

"It's my *only* word. Come back with a warrant or don't come at all."

Halliday nodded, turned his lemonsilla mare away. Thorn followed him and felt a couple of Stant's riders trailing them, no doubt to satisfy the boss that they had left his property.

Halliday kept his voice low-pitched, inaudible to their escorts as he told Thorn, "Jubal's within his rights, and I'm outside my jurisdiction. I can talk to Sheriff Rooney when he gets to Tularosa, tell him what we found, see what he makes of it. Getting a warrant from the county seat is his job. I've already pushed too far."

"No strings on me, though," Gideon replied. "While you go back and make arrangements for your deputy, I'll let these boys turn back, then hang around and see what I can see."

"You've done it this time," Jubal Stant said bitterly. "Leading the dogs right to my door, for Christ's sake!"

Declan fought the urge to smile, saying, "You shouldn't take His name in vain."

His father rounded on him, face tomato-red. "This strike you as a good time to get smart with me, Declan?"

"I'm quoting you, Dad. That's the Third Commandment."

"Even Satan has the power to quote scripture!"

"Hallelujah!"

Jubal spun to slap his son, snarling, but Declan caught his wrist and froze the open hand inches from his left cheek. At six foot five, he had six inches on the old man and outweighed him by a minimum of thirty pounds, two hundred to Jubal's one-seventy or so. Nearly four decades younger and toned from his work on the ranch, Declan's drinking had not yet reduced his brute strength.

"We'll have no more of that," he warned Jubal.

"Goddamn you!"

"Too late."

"Take your hand off of me!"

"Keep your hands to yourself," Declan answered and shoved him away, almost back to his desk.

"You're no damn son of mine," Jubal said.

"Don't you wish that were true?" Declan challenged.

"The redskins destroyed you."

"They brought me to life."

"You call what you do living?"

"I call it my new beginning."

"Christ, the times that I've covered for you!"

"For yourself," Declan sneered. "We can't have your sole heir running wild in the night, can we *Father*?"

"You're not even human."

"You finally begin to understand. The shaman called me *Kilchii*. That's 'Red Boy' to you. Not Indian, but red with blood. I am *Yenaldooshi*, the skinwalker."

"Declan, you've lost your goddamn mind."

"I know it sounds that way to you." He smiled, showing a wide expanse of teeth. "I've fought it too, but that's all over now. Just two more sacrifices and I'm done."

"Done killing?" Jubal almost sounded hopeful, as if it could still be covered up.

"Done with *becoming*," Declan answered. "After that I can go anywhere, be anyone or anything I want to be, forever."

Jubal circled back around his desk and slumped into his tall-backed chair. "How did it come to this?" he asked, deflated now.

"It was my destiny."

"If you believe that—"

"Then I must be crazy. Same old horseshit. Blah-blah-blah."

Declan already knew his father's mind. Jubal kept a Smith & Wesson Model 3 revolver in the top drawer of his desk, on the right side of the knee-well, its cylinder loaded with .44-caliber rounds. He could reach it in an instant, draw and fire, but in his present state Jubal seemed frazzled and disorganized. Declan believed that he was quicker, if not yet invincible. He simply had to time his move precisely, cast off any hesitation at spilling the old man's blood, and get it done.

"I should have left you with them," Jubal said. "The redskins."

"Yes," Declan agreed, closing the gap. "You should have."

"Or the soldiers should have killed you."

"They considered it. I heard them talking. They decided it was best to bring me back."

"Damn fools."

"They couldn't have prevented anything."

"I guess we'll never know."

The drawer eased open half an inch, slid out a little more, and Jubal made a lunge for it. He didn't see the knife slide out of Declan's sleeve or flash across the space between them, sinking deep into his chest. He made a little *oof*ing noise and fell back in his chair, gaping at Declan in surprise.

"This won't take long," Declan advised him, circling around the desk and shoving back his father's chair. He took the Smith & Wesson from its hidey-hole and tucked it underneath his belt, around in back, then stepped between his father's knees and reached down for the knife.

"You always told me Mama was your heart," he said. "But you don't need it anymore."

FIFTEEN

TULAROSA

Heck Halliday found people milling in the street when he returned. His office door was standing open, men and women grouped outside it, looking startled when he nosed his lemonsilla mare in to the hitching rail, climbed down, and loosely tied its reins. The townsfolk parted as he neared the open door. Stepping inside, he spotted Adam Rooney seated in his chair, a deputy perched on the corner of his desk.

"Go on and make yourself at home, Sheriff," said Halliday.

Rooney stayed put, hands clasped over his thick waist, staring back at Halliday. "You weren't here," he replied. "Something about chasing a deputy you lost?"

"He's dead. Butchered like all the rest."

"The hell you say!" Rooney leaned forward, elbows planed on the desktop.

"Hell I don't. You've heard about his horse, no doubt."

"Came in without him."

"And we found him where he camped last night, or what was left of him."

"Who's 'we'?"

"Another fella rode out with me. He's still out there, working on a lead."

"One of your deputies?"

"Not quite."

Rooney gave him hard eyes. Said, "You'd better start at the beginning."

Halliday went through it, starting with the death of Father Luke, his summons to the sheriff, sending Steve Decker to ask for help from Camp Concordia.

"The army?" Rooney challenged. "Why would they horn in on this?"

"Because I asked 'em to," said Halliday. "Because I'm getting nowhere and the same holds true for you."

"Now, just hold on..."

"Hold on to *what*? I've got another five dead since the last time you came up to Tularosa, without any leads to show for it. We're pumpin' dry holes and the murders keep on happening."

"But Heck, the army—"

"Can at least send out patrols and try to keep the killer's head down. More than you or I have managed to accomplish, anyhow."

"We can't be seen to—"

"Fail? What do you think the people have been seeing up to now?"

"Goddamn it!"

"Anyway, I've got a lead. *May* have a lead."

"You wanna share or sit on it and let it hatch?"

Halliday told him about following the tracks from Decker's camp to Jubal Stant's place, how the rancher put them off, demanding that they come back with a warrant if they wanted words with Declan or to have a look around.

"That's your department," he said, finally. "You'd have to wake Judge Passmore up and have him sign the paperwork. Might need more men to make it stick, too."

Rooney waved aside that observation, saying, "Declan Stant. The one snatched by them Navajos ten years ago, or whenever it was?"

"Fifteen. Same boy, all right. Grown up now and a handful for his daddy."

"You think he's the killer?"

"He's the closest to a suspect that we've had so far. Three years with the redskins, in and out of trouble ever since the army brought him home. He and his dad are Catholics—or Declan was, at least—which could link up somehow to the priest's killing."

"*Could* link up *somehow*," said Rooney. "That's nothin' to hang a warrant on, much less a murder charge."

"We won't know till we question him and have a look around the spread for evidence."

"Let's say he killed these folks. You think he carried bits and pieces of 'em home to tuck away?"

"If he's our man, he's crazy as a loon," said Halliday. "No telling what he'd do."

"And daddy, workin' overtime to cover for his boy, would leave 'em all around the house, hither and yon?"

"Until we look—"

"I can't sell that to Passmore. No one could."

"Well, then, you just wasted a trip."

"Seems like it." Rising from behind the desk, Rooney hitched up his trousers. "And forget about the army, Heck. They can't assist civilian lawmen 'less the governor requests it. You should know that."

"Leaving us with what, exactly?"

"If you wanna try'n keep a watch on Declan Stant when he's away from home, go for it. I can approve that much and say it's done on my authority. But don't go trespassin' around his property unless you *see* him try to kill somebody and it's hot pursuit. You hear me?"

"Loud and clear."

"We're gonna have a bite to eat before we head back south. You wanna come along?"

"No thanks. I lost my appetite."

He could have sworn that Rooney smirked at him, a fat man headed off to gain more weight, secure in his office for the next three years. Halliday closed the door behind the sheriff and his deputy, trying to think of who else he could send to Camp Concordia.

Gideon Thorn left Shadow in a grove of cottonwoods and crept up to a brushy hilltop, where he turned his spyglass on the Stant spread down below. The place seemed to have settled since his visit with the marshal, hired hands tending to their business, breaking horses, working in the barn, using the privies as the need arose.

Thorn wasn't sure what to expect. He didn't know if Declan was at home, if Jubal had been consciously protecting him throughout the string of homicides—or even, to a moral certainty, if Declan was responsible. He only knew *someone* had ridden to the ranch from the location where Steve Decker had been killed and grossly mutilated. Someone who found sanctuary there behind the boss man's gruff façade.

And who else would that be, besides the rancher's son

captured by Indians, retrieved after three years a prisoner, and charted on a downward spiral ever since?

Ten minutes or a little more after he found his hiding place, Thorn spotted Declan Stant moving between the farmhouse and the barn. He recognized the young man from his scene on Saturday, outside the Lucky Strike. Thorn didn't recognize the smear of crimson on his chin or matching stains on Declan's hands and shirt, before he ducked into the shady barn.

A couple minutes later, Declan reappeared, seated astride a buckskin stallion. Thorn could not have sworn an oath it was the same horse he had seen on Monday, at the Ostman spread, but it was close enough.

The young man galloped off, ignoring shouted questions from a couple of the hired hands in the dooryard. Thorn tracked him headed north-northwestward, saw one of the ranch hands running for the house, then slipped back to the grove where Shadow waited for him, sensing Thorn's excitement, anxious to be off.

It could be a mistake, following Declan on his own, but Thorn had no means of contacting Marshal Halliday. He'd lose their only suspect and they'd be worse off than when they'd started out that morning, Declan's absence from the homestead scotching any hope they had for a search warrant. He could only trail the man and hope to catch him with incriminating evidence to ring the curtain down.

It took Shadow some time to synchronize with Declan's path of flight. Thorn couldn't follow him too closely, or a backward glance would give the game away and ruin everything. Declan would either turn and fight or, worse yet, strike a pose of injured innocence, pleading harassment by a vengeful lawman and his sidekick, an undeputized civilian.

But if Thorn found Declan with a Henry rifle in his saddle scabbard, that would be a start. Whatever else he found that might link Declan to the murders, that could turn the tide.

As long as he caught Declan off his father's property and made a proper citizen's arrest.

After ten aching minutes, Thorn glimpsed Declan up ahead, three-quarters of a mile away and slowing down now that he'd cleared the ranch. Clearly, the boy knew where he meant to go and he was headed there without a glance behind him to detect any pursuit.

Self-confidence, or did he think he was invincible?

Whatever, Gideon would take advantage of the lapse and trail him all the way, until he found out what in hell was going on.

STANT FARMHOUSE

Foreman Doby Jackson had been barking orders at his hired hands when Declan Stant ran out of the house and into the barn. Stant was a ghastly sight, his shirt and vest blood-speckled, more blood smeared around his lips and chin, with crimson dripping from his hands. Jackson had gaped at him, his first impression that the kid had caught another beating from his father and had maybe paid some of it back in kind. In that scenario he would be running off alone to clear his head, maybe to get stone drunk in Tularosa, so it came as no surprise when he exploded from the barn atop his buckskin stallion, riding like his life depended on it.

Doby had called after him, asked if he needed help, but Declan didn't answer. That was also typical. Next thing the foreman counted on was boss man Jubal raging from the house, calling his son, then angrily demanding to know where he'd gone—as if Doby or any of the other hands could answer that.

But when the old man didn't follow, Jackson wondered what in hell was going on. He knew the pattern of the battles between Jubal and his son as if he were a member of the family, and almost was, as long as he had worked for Jubal Stant. Twelve years now, back when Declan was of school age, still recovering from time spent as a captive of the Navajo.

As if a kid ever really recovered from a thing like that.

Jackson had glimpsed the tattoo markings left on Declan's body by the tribe and wondered to himself, not daring to express it, if the soldiers who had rescued him did a disservice to the boy and to his father both. A bullet in the heat of battle, even called an accident, would have been merciful for all concerned, before the drinking and the other strange behavior came on Declan in his adolescent years.

But right now, Doby's mind was on the boss. Where was he? If there'd been an all-out fight this time, instead of just another beating for the youngster, was the old man injured?

Rushing to the house, he went inside—the door still swinging open, just as Declan left it—and went calling through the rooms, homing on Jubal's study in the north wing. When he found that door ajar as well, he called out "Boss?" one time, then poked his head in—and recoiled from what he saw.

The old man lay stretched out across his desk, his shirt torn open, all awash in blood. His torso was agape, with organs spilling over, and his face was barely recognizable, the features *gnawed* as if by some wild animal. The worst part, if he had to quantify the injuries, was Jubal's heart, removed and set atop his silver belt buckle.

Missing at least one good-sized bite.

Doby couldn't contain his vomit then. He retched until his sides hurt and he knew that he was empty, then lurched back to the front door and out onto the porch. When he could raise his voice, he started shouting to the hands, commanding all of them to saddle up their horses and prepare to follow Declan.

Jubal was—*had been*—a hard man, most particularly on his son, but Doby Jackson still owed him a debt of loyalty, even in death. They'd catch the kid who'd killed him, then decide whether to hang him on their own or take him into Tularosa for the marshal to dispose of. Either way, young Declan had to die for what he'd done.

And as he saddled up his own horse, Doby had to wonder: was this *all* he'd done? Could Declan be behind the other killings that had terrorized Otero County going on a full year and a half?

Why not, after his mind was broken by the Navajo at such an early age?

"Remember, he may have that Henry," Jackson warned the others, as they formed up in the yard. "Longbow, you take the point and figure out his tracks."

Longbow, the broncobuster, was one-fifth Comanche, light enough to pass for white but skilled in tracking and his people's other hunting skills. If anyone could find the fugitive, he was the one.

The hunters galloped off, leaving a haze of dust behind them in the dooryard and the house unoccupied, its door still standing open to the world.

THREE RIVERS, OTERO COUNTY

Declan knows the one and only place where he can hide till nightfall, when he shall begin his last local campaign. Located midway between Tularosa and Carrizozo, the site draws its name from the convergence of three rivers in the Tularosa Basin, at an altitude of forty-five hundred feet in the Sacramento Mountains.

Occupied by aboriginals nine centuries ago, Three Rivers is shunned by most whites as cursed ground, maybe haunted. Lending that impression are some twenty-one thousand petroglyphs—rock carvings of birds, humans, animals, fish, insects and plants, plus various geometric and abstract designs, scattered over fifty acres of the northern Chihuahuan Desert. Declan loves the place, has spent whole days and nights there while he sought the secret of his own survival in a hostile white man's world and gradually understood what is expected of him by the Old Ones.

And it is the perfect place to hide his hunting gear.

This afternoon he rides directly to the crevice where he keeps his costume hidden, knowing it is safe. A coral snake guards his stash, packing sufficient venom to kill half a dozen men, but Declan has no fear of lifting it aside and hauling out the items he requires. A sturdy shake to clear out any lurking scorpions or spiders, and he lays the gear aside, scoops up the brightly-colored snake, and places it back in the shade.

"All yours," he says, and smiles. "I won't be coming back."

His future lies elsewhere, but first he has a final sweep to make. He must leave Tularosa a reminder of his presence there, to pass down through the generations in hushed tones. A night of bloodletting with no full moon, as *Yenal-dooshi* takes his leave and goes ... well, anywhere he likes.

The town itself shall be his final sacrifice, in case his father doesn't count somehow.

It does not matter that the ranch hands will accuse him, that the law will bar him from inheriting his father's property and fortune. Declan has enough cash in his pocket to get by for now, and more will always be available. *Yenal-dooshi* is cunning. He knows tricks that dazzle mortal men and leave them baffled, wondering what happened to their money, wives and families.

That is, if they are still alive.

Eyes closed, his face uptilted toward the sun, Declan imagines a vast map of all the states and territories in the West. He can go anywhere, do anything. For all he knows his lifespan may be infinite. If not immortal, he will certainly outlive the other men around him by decades. They have no power over him, and while he suffered wounds on one occasion—at the hardware store in town— that was *before* his transformation to another plane.

He trusts the shamans who explained all this to him so long ago, before the soldiers came.

Before he knows it, Declan—*Yenaldooshi now*—is chanting, dancing short and choppy steps he learned by observation with the tribe. No one is there to criticize if he makes a mistake, places a foot wrong. Anyway, it is the spirit of the thing that matters, offering the remnant of his soul up to the Old Gods in exchange for their protection and infusion of their power.

Making him invincible.

He waits for darkness, since it is his element, but he can still prepare before the sun goes down. Shedding his blood-stained white-man's clothes, he dons the sacred costume one piece at a time, adjusting it, feeling the skin *merge* with his own in affirmation of his nature that invigorates him.

Finished, he begins to dance again, more energetic and enthusiastic now. The power of Three Rivers flows into his body from the stone beneath his feet, raising his hair in tingling bristles. Chanting to the sky, then howling like the animal he shall become, *Yenaldooshi* welcomes his surrender to the Other Side.

SIXTEEN

THREE RIVERS, OTERO COUNTY

Gideon Thorn kept his quarry in sight while Declan, on his buckskin, climbed the desert's rising ground toward rocky outcrops on the skyline. Shadow labored slightly, but the stallion's strength prevailed, staying about two hundred yards behind the fugitive at Thorn's mental command. Only when they were closing on the pinnacle did Thorn lose sight of Stant and slow his gray to a walk, then a halt.

Already they were ringed by scattered stones, grown thicker as the slopes rose toward their pinnacle above. Thorn glanced around and saw the nearest of them scored by ancient carvings, granite surfaces marked with what seemed, respectively, to be a hawk's or eagle's head in profile, something like a leaping bighorn ram, a human hand with fingers splayed, and symbols he could not define: a circle with a cross inside it, ringed by little boxes; squiggly lines that might mean anything from wind to rivers down below; zigzags that might be taken for a lightning storm.

Above him, where the fleeing youth and buckskin horse had disappeared, the marked stones marched away in files and clusters, ranging from the size of dinner plates to man-sized stones and larger, most of them displaying artwork from the first tribe that had colonized the Tularosa Basin. Thorn had no idea how old they were and, at the moment, did not care. He only knew that Declan Stant had found himself an aerie with no end of hiding places if he left his animal and went to ground.

Which meant Thorn had to do the same.

"Wait here," he told Shadow, and reinforced it with a silent message via thought. The horse was smart enough to flee from danger if it came too close, or fight back with its kicking, slashing hooves if it surprised him.

Stant removed the Winchester repeater from its saddle boot and started up the hill on foot. He marked the spot where Declan Stant had dropped from sight but knew his adversary might have traveled fifty yards by then, crouching and armed with anything from bare hands to the Henry he'd been wielding in the village Sunday night. He still could not explain the blood on Declan's face and hands when he had fled the farmhouse, but it was irrelevant, much like the import of the stones surrounding Thorn.

The young man he was stalking had already murdered nineteen people that he knew of for a certainty, and Thorn was not about to make it twenty through an act of carelessness.

He started climbing, hot in his black suit but grateful for the hat that cast shade on his face and neck. Around him, in the waning afternoon, shadows from the innumerable stones were growing longer, slanting to eastward if he needed a reminder of which way his path was taking him. His Winchester was fully loaded but he left its hammer down, in case he stumbled in his climb, thereby avoiding any accidental shots.

Did Declan know he was pursued or who was chasing him? For all Thorn knew, the killer could have picked this spot from other visits in the past, some personal affinity for points held sacred by the territory's first inhabitants. Was it related in some way to his captivity by Navajos, something that had impressed his mind during the three years he had been their helpless prisoner?

Again, Thorn dropped the train of thought as an irrelevancy and distraction from his hunt.

Whatever Declan Stant might think or feel, that was a matter for the county court, perhaps influenced by whatever alienists could be found to plead his case for innocence by reason of insanity. Thorn knew the basics of that rule as it applied in the United States—a proven inability by a defendant to distinguish "right" from "wrong" as understood by so-called civilized society—and none of that meant anything while Stant was still at large, still killing innocents.

Ideally, Thorn wanted to speak with Declan and persuade him to surrender voluntarily, but that seemed so unlikely that he virtually put it out of mind. If there was time and opportunity he'd speak his piece, but he had come prepared to kill in self-defense and in defense of the community that had already suffered so much loss.

Not for the first time, Thorn suspected that his trail would end in death.

The trick was to make sure that it was not his own.

Doby Jackson's posse followed Longbow over scrub and barren desert, making toward the Sacramento Mountains at a gallop. Their mixed-breed guide had shown no hesitation yet, following tracks that he'd described as clear-cut from the time they left the Stant spread, leading in a more or less straight line as if the boss man's son and murderer could not imagine he would be pursued.

Or maybe that he didn't give a damn.

All of the hands but one had joined the chase. Doby had noticed Early Gibson missing from the pack of nineteen others when they formed up in the barnyard, but he hadn't bothered calling for the straggler, simply made a mental note to deal with him when they returned if Gibson had the bad sense to remain after he'd skipped the most important job he'd ever have. Nineteen was plenty to collect Declan and vote as to his disposition, with the mood already leaning toward a necktie party for the crime that threatened all their futures, not to mention stealing all those lives that he'd cut short.

As Doby thought about it, following the part-Injun and eating trail dust, he supposed a hanging was unlikely. Even if he was oblivious to their pursuit, Declan must know his hours were numbered as a free man. When he saw their party coming, he would have to run or fight, and from what Jackson had observed in Jubal Stant's study, the kid was puredee loco, cracked, long gone around the bend. No reason why he wouldn't make a stand against their posse, most particularly if he had his Henry rifle with him when he fled the ranch.

The hands all knew that and accepted danger as a part of what they'd come to do. It wasn't simply bagging Declan and deciding whether they should put him down or hand him over to the law in Tularosa; it was also risking life and limb to get it done, same way they ran a risk of injury or death when they were herding cows or breaking wild broncs from the range. A cowboy's life was hard and often short.

But rarely did they come upon a human monster like their boss man's crazy son.

It wouldn't be much longer till their horses had to slow and rest awhile, walking instead of galloping flat-out beneath the lowering but still intensely brutal sun. If they were left afoot through loss of animals, Declan would probably escape, and that came down to Doby Jackson. It would be *his* fault, not Longbow's or the others', if they lost their man by riding too damned hard and long without a respite.

As if his thought had reached their guide, Longbow reined in and raised a hand. The other riders swirled around him, Doby half expecting Longbow to announce he'd lost the killer's trail. Instead, the scout looked Jackson in the eye and said, "Three Rivers."

"What about it?" Doby asked.

"That's where he's headed to."

"The hell is that?" one of the new men, Augie Gruber, asked.

"Old Injun place," Longbow replied, as if he wasn't one of them himself. "Carvings on many rocks."

"And 'bout a million places he could hide to pick us off," said Doby, cursing a blue streak inside his head.

Some of the others muttered, looking sour. They had either seen Three Rivers or had heard about it and were picturing themselves pinned down by rifle fire from somewhere on the heights, trying to get an angle on their man while he was peering down their throats. Doby knew how they felt, but fear was something to be overcome, not cultivated in a man with any self-respect.

"We've got another hour, maybe hour and a quarter till we get there," he announced. "We'll walk the horses for ten minutes now, then finish it. If any of you want to drop out, now's the time. Go back and wait till I get there to pay your severance. Whoever stays with me, we're goin' on."

He didn't take a vote, just gave a nod to Longbow and the guide continued on his way, charting the course, with Doby close behind him. Pride made Jackson wait five minutes before glancing back across his shoulder, verifying that the other seventeen were all still with him, following his lead.

Whatever waited for them at Three Rivers, they were going into it together like the Frenchman wrote it: all for one and one for all.

TULAROSA

Without the county sheriff breathing down his neck and telling him what not to do, Heck Halliday was trying to regain control. He'd gone first to the Lucky Strike and called for volunteers to ride to Camp Concordia. It was a hard sell, with the word about Steve Decker's death and then his body coming in, covered in canvas, in the back of Josiah Groom's wagon, but two men raised their hands at last and Halliday had picked the one who wasn't stinking drunk.

With that done and a half day wasted, still no guarantee the army would respond at all, Halliday walked back to his office, wondering what Thorn was up to at the Stant place. There was no way Halliday could ride back out and hope to find him, so he scratched that notion off his list and found that he had nothing to replace it with.

He felt stymied, as if his hands were tied. The sheriff wouldn't help him move on Jubal Stant, despite the clues that pointed to Stant's son, and Jubal, for his part, still seemed intent on heading up a search for the "real killer" that could set out anytime, perhaps grabbing some hapless drifter whom they'd blame for all the killings just to clean the slate.

Halliday cursed his impotence and wondered what the use was even carrying a badge, when laws conspired against him punishing the guilty or investigating prime suspects. He understood the basic Bill of Rights but also saw them as a stumbling block to lawmen in a wild land where the law was bent and broken constantly, often with only one man like himself to ride herd on a whole community. It might not qualify as anarchy per se, but it was getting pretty goddamned close.

No sooner had he dropped into the chair behind his desk than Halliday heard someone shouting for him in the street outside. He rose, was halfway to his open door, when he beheld a rider pulling up outside his office in a swirl of dust, dismounting, quickly tying off his horse's reins. The man was someone Halliday believed he'd seen before, maybe in passing on the street—or had it been more recently, when he and Thorn confronted Jubal Stant?

"Marshal," the breathless rider said, "I'm Early Gibson."

"And?"

"I ride for Jubal Stant, or did."

"What's that mean?"

"He's been kilt," said Gibson. "Gutted in his own house, by his own boy.'

"*What?*"

"You heard me right, Marshal. A short time after you was out there with that other fella, Declan come runnin' out of the house all bloody, like he hugged a side o' beef or somethin'. Went straight to the barn and came out on his buckskin, ridin' hard."

Buckskin. The Ostman place.

"That wouldn't be a stallion?" he asked Gibson.

"Damn sure is. So, after he rid off, ol' Doby—that's the foreman—run inside the house to parlay with the boss man, and he come back out a second later, sayin' Mr. Stant was dead and Declan kilt him. Cut him all to pieces on his desk, if you'd believe it, and his heart..."

Gibson stopped short, looked sickly. Halliday snapped at him, "Spit it out!"

" 'Cording to Doby, somebody'd been *chewing* on it."

"Jesus! Where's he now?"

"Dunno," Gibson replied. "He rid off, like I said, and after Doby saw the boss man, he collected ever'body else to chase the son."

"But you begged off?"

"Didn't say nothin', just hung back and let 'em go. The way they talked, I knew they planned on killin' 'im if they could catch 'im. I seen a lynchin' once, Marshal. It put me off the vigilante way."

"So, you have no idea where they were headed?"

"North-northwest is all I know for sure, like towards the Sacramento range. Doby had Eddie Longbow leadin' 'em. He's part Injun and good at trackin' cattle, men, whatever."

"Damn it all to hell!"

Gibson moved back a step. "Marshal, I come straight here, quick as I could, and—"

Halliday held up a calming hand. "It's not your fault. You want to, tell 'em at the Lucky Strike I'll stand you to a whiskey and a beer. One round, mind you."

"Yessir! And thank you, sir! If I knew any more—"

"Go on, now. I've got things to do."

Like what? a voice inside his head demanded. He could try

to form another posse, but to what end? Stant's ranch lay outside his jurisdiction, as the sheriff had reminded him. So did the Sacramento Mountains, and he couldn't scour them effectively in any case, not even if the whole town rode with him to help. Without some indication where the Stant boy might be headed, all that Halliday could do was send another messenger to Sheriff Rooney, tell him what had happened, and sit waiting until he returned, most likely in the morning.

Not for the first time, Halliday felt completely useless, sick of carrying his badge in vain.

THREE RIVERS

Yenaldooshi sniffs the wind and growls. He smells a horse, its rider, and a hint of danger to himself. Nothing to fret about, since he is breaking free, swiftly coming into his own, but still an opposition that he cannot tolerate. It does not worry him, but rather stirs his blood, preparing him for battle.

Yenaldooshi, formerly a boy called Declan Stant, is more than simply man or beast now, a transcendent fusion of the two. His body has assumed its proper form with fur, talons and fangs, but he retains the wisdom of his human mind, enhanced by interaction with the shaman long ago. All that his master taught him, all he's learned since then, is part and parcel of the fearsome whole. He knows men, knows their strengths and weaknesses, knows how to use their tools.

The Henry rifle, for example. He can wield it like a marksman, though his last attempt at sniping, carried out in purely human form, was not a great success. Today is different, a man pursuing *Yenaldooshi* in his primal form, on sacred ground. The fool must have a death wish, and it is about to be fulfilled.

He moves downhill, taking his time and following his nose, picking the larger stones to cover him from being spotted until he is ready. When the battle has been joined, he counts on his appearance as another weapon in his arsenal, to shock the hunter who has come for him.

One of his late and unlamented father's men, perhaps. It matters not to *Yenaldooshi*, since from this day forward, men are simply prey to him. He need not bargain with them, live by their rules in the daylight, cater to their whims. It is *their* lot to live in fear of *him*, as it was meant to be from ages past.

Away down slope, his eyes pick out a figure all in black, making his cautious way uphill. It is the stranger whom he tried to kill in Tularosa, giving him a second chance. That knowledge chills him, but it is not fear. Rather, he notes it as excitement, a prelude to sacrifice.

Crouching behind a stone slab decorated with a serpent and a human profile, *Yenaldooshi* aims along the Henry's barrel, easing back the rifle's hammer with his thumb.

SEVENTEEN

The flat *crack* of a rifle shot echoed loud among the countless stones around Gideon Thorn. He ducked immediately, but the slug had missed already, spraying chips of granite from a slab some inches to his left, stinging his cheek and peppering his high-crowned hat.

A slip had saved him, Thorn's left boot sliding a little back and downward, dropping him a crucial inch or two below the sniper's line of sight. If he'd been more sure-footed, if he'd risen for a peek over the stones around him, he'd be down, a clean hole through his head to snuff out conscious thought.

Beyond the obvious, uphill, Thorn couldn't say exactly where the shot had come from. That it was not followed up immediately by a second gave him pause, and hope. He hesitated to reveal himself, knowing the shooter would be waiting for another chance, but also realized the gunman could not see him where he was, hunkered behind a decorated boulder that depicted leaping deer.

But simply hiding out was not an option. Thorn had to proceed uphill and find his man, which left a choice of moving to his left or right. The left-hand path would place him in a kind of aisle between two rows of standing stones, their glyphs that he could see from where he crouched pointed downhill to welcome climbers or deter them from ascending. To his right, the granite blocks were staggered, forcing him to run what Harvard's football coach would call a broken-field pattern, ducking back and forth around the obstacles, perhaps while under fire.

Thorn made his choice and rolled out to the right, preferring partial cover to the long, clear lane that opened on his left, a funnel where he might be trapped and cut down from above. The first shot came when he had barely cleared his hiding place, the bullet whining past him with a few inches to spare. Thorn thumbed his rifle's hammer back and fired a snap shot from the waist, not aiming, almost instantly rewarded with the slap of lead on stone.

A miss, as he'd expected, but at least the sniper knew this time they were on fairly equal ground and similarly armed. It was a showdown to the finish. Only one of them —if that—would walk away.

Somewhere off to Thorn's left, westward toward the setting sun, a hawk took flight, screeching. Dusk was approaching, a mixed blessing if he took for granted that his quarry knew the ground while he did not. It would be different in darkness, even with the light of a third quarter moon to help Thorn navigate. It might as well have been the landscape of some other planet, where he stalked a monster in the dark.

As if to emphasize that point, a loud, coarse howling warbled through the hills, held for a moment, then descended into snarling. Thorn repressed a shudder at the sound, the memories it conjured for him, taking full advantage of the spreading shadows as he edged his way uphill.

And then, after the howl, a nearly human voice: "You want me? Come and get me!"

To Thorn, although he'd only heard the young man speak in drunken tones before, it sounded as if Declan's mouth had *changed,* sprouted more teeth than any human should possess, bridging the gap between a man and animal.

What kind? And was it even possible?

Those were the questions he had ridden north from Mexico to answer. No fear of the creeping darkness or its brute inhabitant could stop him now. Fate had directed Gideon to this place, at this time, and he would see it through at any cost.

It was his choice. His destiny.

And he would meet it head-on, with his eyes wide-open. Facing death.

Yenaldooshi moves on bare and silent feet, heedless of jagged rocks beneath his calloused soles. Night is descending, his old friend and fond accomplice to his sacrifices. This night will observe his final transformation into what he's been becoming over time, by slow degrees, despite his father's fruitless efforts to defer what is ordained.

Something comes to mind, drilled into him from one of Shakespeare's plays by teachers who are heedless of his true identity: *What fools these mortals be.*

He does not know the man in black beyond his name, a stranger come to hunt him down for motives *Yenaldooshi* does not grasp beyond the obvious. Some men kill anything they do not understand, or which will not bend to their will. They stand at odds with Nature and the Old Gods, seeking in their arrogance to rule a world much older and more complex than they dare to dream. They need a "holy book" of myths to circumscribe the Earth and justify their futile efforts to despoil it. When confronted even with a sliver of the truth, a glimmer of what lies beyond, they quake and quail, pleading for mercy in the final seconds of their lives.

Yenaldooshi doesn't know whether the man in black will plead, but he can bleed and die. That much is certain. It is *Yenaldooshi*'s pleasure to remind him of that fact and to devour his heart, his inner strength, as culmination of his final sacrifice. Before his death, the man in black will see and understand.

Yenaldooshi descends. He hears and feels his fur brushing against the stones with all their etchings, but the sound is muffled, nothing to betray him with the night breeze sighing steadily cross Three Rivers. This will be his first kill made on sacred ground, a fitting tribute to the tribesmen of so long ago who made this place their temple to the moon and stars.

He almost sets the Henry down, then thinks better of that and keeps it with him. Even with his present strength, *Yenaldooshi* cannot be certain he is bulletproof. Until this final sacrifice has been completed, he cannot be absolutely sure of that.

But afterward...

He sniffs the wind, picks up the scent he's looking for, and changes his direction. It is marvelous, the way his senses serve him in this guise. *Yenaldooshi* hopes that in the future they will operate as ably when he is in human form, as when he changes to reveal his truer self. It must be marvelous to see for miles, to scent a packrat deep inside its burrow, and to hear the whisper of a snake's scales over sand.

His brotherhood with Nature, soon to be complete.

Trailing the man's scent, *Yenaldooshi* soon picks out the sound of boots on stone, as well. He cannot see his quarry yet, but knows approximately where he is, climbing to reach the summit while his nemesis, unseen, comes down to intercept him.

If the man in black knew he was coming, would he turn and run? It would not save him now, but *Yenaldooshi* wonders if he has the grit to stand and face his end when it arrives, or if he'll soil himself like others in the past and plead in vain for mercy that is not forthcoming. In his heart and in his beast brain, *Yenaldooshi* hopes the man will make a decent fight of it, despite the fact that he is doomed to lose.

He knows the outcome in advance, and counts on it, but *Yenaldooshi* still wants it to be a contest worthy of his strength, his cunning. Otherwise, why not just tear a rabbit limb from limb and count it as a worthy sacrifice?

Besides the man in black's fear sweat, he smells gun oil —a given in the circumstances, when only a fool would come at him unarmed. Glad now that he still has the Henry, fourteen rimfire rounds remaining in its magazine and chamber, he slips forward, lips drawn back from teeth designed to ravage flesh and bone.

Unable to resist, he tilts his head back toward the rising moon and howls.

APPROACHING THREE RIVERS

First one rifle shot, then two more echoing across the flats in rapid-fire. That means two weapons and a battle joined, though silence falls across the landscape once again, dusk lowering to mask the trail that Doby Jackson's party had been following.

No matter. They were close enough to find Three Rivers now, even without Longbow to guide them in. Doby had been there once before and knew the landmarks, weathering by slow degrees through eons, nothing in the way of changes that would catch the naked eye.

Somewhere up there was Declan Stant—and someone else. Doby had no idea if it was Marshal Halliday, the man who had accompanied him to the ranch that afternoon, or someone else. Nor did he care. Someone was after Declan, which meant one more gun on Doby's side when they arrived.

Unless the stranger was already dead by then.

In any case, he would be slowing Declan down, and that was good enough.

"Come on!" he urged the others, as he spurred his mount back to a gallop for the final quarter-mile. The others snapped their reins or shouted at their horses, joining in the rush as if it were the last leg of a race, craving the purse.

In this case, they were chasing justice—or revenge, the proper name was unimportant. Either way, it ended with their boss man's slayer dead: shot down, strung up, or held for trial and hanged by lawful means.

And that was all that Doby Jackson cared about.

He hadn't been that fond of Jubal Stant but owed him something all the same, a steady job and decent treatment through the years, although he sometimes bore the brunt of Jubal's pent-up wrath at Declan's antics, at the weather, at most anything Doby could name. More to the point, his death was *savage*, sickening, not just a knockdown accident during a fight between an overbearing father and his wayward son. It was the latest in a string of murders that would straggle on indefinitely if the madman were not brought to heel.

Over the sound of clopping hoofbeats, Doby shouted to the other men, "Be ready with them guns when we get there. No tellin' what we're like to find."

And then the howling came, a coughing, wailing sound unlike what any of the hands had heard from coyotes or wolves before. Longbow reined in his mount and glanced over at Doby, the others unsettled and milling about while awaiting their foreman's command. Ashamed of the chill that had raced down his spine, Doby turned it around, lashing out at the hired hands.

"We knew he was crazy," he snapped. "Now he's howling like some kinda mad dog. What of it? He's still flesh and blood, nothin' but!"

"You sure a that?" Zell Mudgett asked. "That didn't sound human to me!"

"You gonna tell me you believe in wolfmen?" Doby answered back. "I want a show of hands from everyone who still believes in fairy tales. Right now!"

None of their hands went up, but several of their shadowed faces turned away. Doby sat waiting for another moment, then told all of them, "I'm goin' on. Whoever wants to quit, turn back just like I said before. You'll get your severance as soon as I get back to settle up Jubal's affairs. Last thing I need is cowards ridin' on my heels."

With that, he spurred his animal and set off on the final gallop to Three Rivers, just a couple hundred yards now, where he'd have to leave his mount and do the rest on foot. He damn sure wasn't looking forward to that part of it, but turning back wasn't an option. And his riders seemed to feel the same. Reluctant as they might be, they were coming on behind him, some already drawing rifles from their saddle boots as they approached the rock pile and its howling occupant.

THREE RIVERS

Gideon Thorn heard the rush coming, panting breath and footfalls first, giving him time to duck behind a granite slab before the bullets started flying wild, the unseen Henry's lever-action *clack-clack-clacking* as his enemy ejected brass, pumping a new round up into the rifle's chamber every second and a half or so. He tried to count the rounds, knowing that even with a reload there could only be sixteen, hoping the first two had not been replaced before the charge—and sure enough, after fourteen the gun fell silent.

Not so, its possessor.

Now, instead of blazing shots in rapid fire, Declan was snarling like an animal, still hurtling downhill, toward the last place he'd have caught a glimpse of Thorn. Gideon rose to meet him, startled by how close the young man was, but still squeezed off an aimed shot from his Winchester before a big hand struck the gun and knocked it from his hands.

No, not a hand precisely. It had *claws*, and there was fur all up the length of Declan's arm. In fact, as Thorn recoiled, he saw his adversary was completely cloaked in fur, the thick skin of an animal or more than one, whatever it or they might be. A leering bear's head perched on top of Declan's skull, the youngster's human face seeming to peer out from between its open jaws, surrounded by its fangs. A smaller set of teeth, perhaps a wolf's, had somehow sprouted on the *inside* of Stant's mouth, making coherent speech impossible, but still allowing him to hoot and growl.

Clawed hands lashed out at Thorn, one of them knocking off his hat, and he tipped over backward, rolled away from Declan with the trained agility of Engolo ritual combat, learned at the knee of Obi Magoro. He came up crouching, drew his right-hand Colt, and fanned two shots at point-blank range before another sweep of talons drove him back and down, another shoulder roll to keep himself beyond the madman's killing reach.

Both shots went home and Declan staggered, but he came back strong, powered by rage and his insanity. His arms windmilled, the bear claws fastened to his hands slicing the air. Thorn fired again, aiming for Declan's heart by pale moonlight, then ducked and dodged another sweep of talons stained with human blood.

Declan was slowing, staggering, but still upright, still bellowing, though with a deep, wet gurgle in his voice now. He advanced, the wolf teeth clacking in his mouth, eyes glazed with rage or pain or some of both, intent on disemboweling the pursuer who had wounded him. He still had strength enough, from all appearances, to do the job.

Thorn stood his ground this time, lifted the Colt to full arm's length, and fired his fourth shot through the gleaming bear's fangs, into Declan Stant's forehead. The eerie double-head snapped back, its owner frozen for a moment in mid-stride, and then he toppled slowly over backwards, landing in a bulky heap.

Thorn took his time approaching Stant, surveying him by moonlight. Now he saw that Declan wore a full bear's skin over his naked skin, its forelegs fastened to his wrists and biceps, while its rear legs were attached to his at thighs and ankles, with the beast's claws overlapping his bare feet.

It was the pelt of what had been a fair-sized grizzly, large enough to kill and eat a cow or man. Beneath it, strange tattoos marked Declan's bloodstained chest and abdomen.

Madness, Thorn told himself, *but nothing supernatural.*

There was no answer to his private torment here.

Voices from down below stirred Gideon out of his reverie. He drew his second Peacemaker and turned to face the sounds, saw men ascending toward the spot where he stood over Declan's corpse.

"Hold up there!" one of them called out to him. "We're after Declan Stant!"

"You're late," Thorn answered back. "But come ahead."

EPILOGUE

TULAROSA: JUNE 24, 1875

Thorn stayed an extra day and night in Tularosa, helping Marshal Halliday sort out the loose ends of his case. The county sheriff came again and muttered vague displeasure, but could find no fault with the conclusion of the homicides and rode back home to Alamogordo, doubtless pondering how he could claim the credit for himself. Late on June twenty-third, six soldiers under the command of a young first lieutenant came from Camp Concordia, received word that they were no longer needed, and repaired to drinking at the Lucky Strike before they turned around and left again on Thursday morning, all of them the worse for booze, but with a story they could share.

Josiah Groom retrieved the corpse of Declan Stant, and Thorn attended his examination with Heck Halliday and Myron Colfax, who did not forget his camera. The body, when undressed completely, with a set of cunningly designed wolf's teeth extracted from its jaws, was found to bear tattoos which Halliday identified as Navajo spanning its chest, stomach, and back. Based on distortion of the patterns over time, they'd been applied during the years when Declan was a tribal captive, never mentioned by the young man or his father in the intervening years.

Halliday thought the tattoos had something to do with Nature and the Navajo religion. Colfax photographed them all, determined to investigate it with an expert of his personal acquaintance, somewhere in the East. Already planning out a series of exclusive articles, the newsman seemed to think Stant's story would be worth a book once he compiled all of the details and had time to write it down.

Gideon Thorn happily left him to it, asking only that his own role in the case not be exaggerated in the style of certain dime novels he'd seen, transforming outlaws into heroes and reducing other real-life persons to pathetic caricatures of themselves. In fact, he'd likely never read it and would live with whatever the editor produced, oblivious to the percent of fiction mixed with fact.

And in his chosen line of work, publicity was not always a detriment.

For his final breakfast in the village, Thorn entered the Lucky Strike at half-past six a.m. and was astounded when the six or seven diners there before him rose as one, applauding him, while one of the men shouted, "Bravo!" Close to blushing, he followed the morning waitress to a table by the front window and nodded thanks when she told him, "It's on the house, with thanks."

Feeling he had no choice, Thorn ordered three fried eggs with ham, grilled mushrooms on the side, a short stack of pancakes, and coffee. After eating every bite and quaffing down a second mug of java, he made sure to tip the waitress even though he wasn't paying for the meal, then went out shopping for supplies to carry on the trail. He bought beef jerky, hardtack, beans and coffee, bundled all that up, and then found his attempt to pay rejected for the second time that morning, settled with a hearty "thank-you" from the village grocer and a wish, perhaps even sincere, that he would favor Tularosa with another visit sometime in the future.

Marshal Halliday was waiting for him at the livery, smiling and telling Thorn, "I didn't want to interrupt another of your meals. That's a bad habit that I'm working on."

"Your timing's perfect," Thorn assured him.

"I just want to thank you once more for your help—well, more than help, God knows—wrapping this whole thing up. For what it's worth, and I'm not sure that's anything, I have a feeling this election's in the bag."

"They could do worse," Thorn said. "The Stants?"

"They're being planted on the ranch this afternoon, on either side of Jubal's wife. I'd hate to be around on Judgment Day. You want to come?"

"I'll pass. Who takes over the spread?" Thorn asked.

"A nice surprise for Doby Jackson. You remember him?"

"He led the riders after Declan. Showed up late."

"That's him. In Jubal's will he listed Doby next in line, after the son, if Declan couldn't run the spread for any reason. No specifics mentioned, but we know now what he had in mind. So Doby's rich, I guess, and never saw it coming."

The hostler brought Shadow, leaving Thorn to saddle up the gray as usual, then went to fetch Bell from her stall next to the stallion's. By the time Gideon had the tack and saddle squared away it was pushing eight o'clock.

"Mind if I ask you where you're going next?" Halliday

posed the question without any sense of irony at asking it before permission had been granted.

"It's a toss-up," Thorn replied, thinking about the clippings he'd reviewed on Wednesday night, while Tularosans celebrated at the Lucky Strike and spilled into the street. "There have been children disappearing two-by-two in the vicinity of Hayden Butte, in Arizona Territory. Farther north, up in Nevada, people at Pahrump claim there's some kind of creature wandering around they can't describe. That's thin, but they've reported some attacks on livestock that could be related. If I head the other way, farmers around Waco have been reporting odd activity by animals."

"Livestock again?" asked Halliday.

"And wildlife, too. Seems anything that walks or crawls has been attacking people for no reason."

"Always something."

"And the list keeps growing."

"Has it helped you yet, at all, about the business with your family?"

"Not yet," Thorn said. "But I keep hoping."

"Well, I guess I'm foolish saying it, but if you're ever passing through this way again..."

"You never know," Thorn said.

"I'll leave you to it, then. Good-by."

They shook hands and the marshal left as Bell arrived, trailing the hostler. Thorn saw to her packing for the trail and silently assured her that they wouldn't push it, wherever they wound up traveling. Bell took it in, blinked once, and almost seemed to smile.

Of course, mules couldn't shrug.

Thorn paid the hostler, mounted up, and left the livery with Bell pacing along Shadow's left flank. He had been

truthful, telling Halliday he didn't know where they were
going next. He thought he'd let the road decide, when they
were clear of Tularosa and its ghosts.

There was no shortage in the West of mysteries
remaining to be solved.

A LOOK AT: LEVIATHAN RISING (GIDEON THORN 2)

Gideon Thorn is no stranger to monsters. Since the day his family was slaughtered by an inhuman predator, he's wandered the West, chasing the impossible—and hunting the unknowable. But nothing could prepare him for what's rising in the arid wastes of southwest Texas.

When reports surface of a massive, man-eating creature freed from the depths of a silver mine, Thorn rides into a town on the brink of collapse. The skies are no longer safe, bodies are piling up, and the townsfolk live in fear of what flies above. But danger doesn't just come on leathery wings —on the ground, a ruthless robber baron backed by Pinkertons threatens to crush anyone in his way, including the strong-willed widow fighting to save her home.

Caught between a monstrous predator and a brutal human enemy, Thorn must unravel the mystery before the nightmare claims everything—and everyone. The West has never been wilder...or deadlier.

AVAILABLE OCTOBER 2025

ABOUT THE AUTHOR

A California native, Michael Newton published over 215 books under his own name and various pseudonyms since 1977. He began writing professionally as a "ghost" for author Don Pendleton on the best-selling Executioner series. With 104 episodes published to date, Newton nearly tripled the number of Mack Bolan novels completed by creator Pendleton himself.

www.ingramcontent.com/pod-product-compliance
Lightning Source LLC
Chambersburg PA
CBHW020644260626
47157CB00008B/2905